FALLEN ANGELS SING

OMAR TORRES

Arte Publico Press
Houston
Texas
1991

This volume is made possible through a grant from the National Endowment for the Arts, a federal agency.

Arte Publico Press
University of Houston
Houston, Texas 77204-2090

Cover design by Mark Piñón
Cover art by Jorge Hernández Porto

Torres, Omar, 1945–
    Fallen Angels Sing / Omar Torres.
        p.   cm.
    ISBN 1-55885-024-4
    1. Cuba—History—Revolution, 1959—Fiction. I.
Title. PS3570.0699F35 1990
813'.54–dc20   90-38830

                                                        CIP

The paper used in this publication meets the minimum requirements of the American National Standard for Permanence of Paper for Printed Library Materials Z39.48-1984. ∞

Copyright © 1991 by Omar Torres
Printed in the United States of America

For Niurka

He went out, not knowing whither he went.

HEBREUS, 11–8

You don't have to forsee the future, but to allow it ...

SAINT-EXUPERY, in *Citadelle*

Without memory, nostalgia passes for history.

RICHARD STENGEL

It's an old Gnostic tradition that we don't invent things, we just remember.

ROBERT BLY

Either I am nobody, or I am a nation.

DEREK WALCOTT

Fallen Angels Sing

THREE STEPS AND A SHUFFLE

There is an island where the last surviving Indian chieftain was given the choice of either going to heaven—together with the Spanish conquistadors—or being burned at the stake, and he chose the latter. It is an island of which the creator of Surrealism said is too surrealist a place to live in; an island where men have always been willing to die for history and live for the moment; an island of women who, requiring passion, love and attention, and while suffering the consequences of machismo, want their men to be machos; an island where nothing is sacred, nothing taken seriously; an island of familiarity, of games; an island where everyone speaks in diminutives, where oratory is of utmost importance, and gregariousness the order of the day; an island where a man's voice can start a revolution, and often has; an island of improvisation, of subtle discrimination; an island of excessive sensibility and intense melancholy; an island, I've been told, where someone has seen my shadow.

CANVAS WITH DEMONS AND CHERUBIMS

Death was never one of my fears, but that never kept it from dancing in my mind. Countless times I tried to imagine not being anymore, but the idea of being separated from the memory of my friends, from the touch of their words and the warmth of their embrace made me shiver. What I never conceived was that my life would end the way it did.

January 2nd, 1979. In the center of Revolution Square, the monumental statue to José Martí would once again witness the bizarre behavior of its people.

I met the sculptor of José Martí's statue, Juan José Sicre, in New York some years back. He was a short, bespectacled, taciturn, septuagenarian with a tender smile. We didn't really know him at the time; we were young and displaced, with an urge to find our roots. Honoring a well-known artist from an older generation seemed a sensible way to begin our journey. We were trying to verify our continuity by recovering our culture, by holding on to all that seemed positive, while shunning what we saw as embarrassing or detrimental.

In New York, we called our compatriots living in Miami "Cubanoids" because they wore huge chains, medals and link bracelets, all of 18K gold; because they liked big cars and extravagant homes; because in a corner of a room in their houses they kept preposterous altars of African deities with a plethora of food, flowers, money, candles and desperate beliefs; because they went on Sunday picnics to the beach with pot after pot of rice and beans and roast pork; because they rehashed worn-out political slogans; because they patronized over-lit, mirrored restaurants more to be seen than to eat; and because they had resurrected pre-Castro Cuba on Miami's Southwest 8th Street.

We, on the other hand, were little Latin snobs living in New

York, locked-up in crowded rooms, trying to survive the weather and the isolation; an unnatural life for children of the tropics, worshippers of sun and song. We wore the latest St. Laurent, went to Broadway, the opera, to concerts. Summers were, of course, spent in Europe. We read best sellers and *The New York Times* while keeping up-to-date with all the frivolities of the moment.

After a half-year pilgrimage, I was convinced of having exhausted all exits, all escapes, all excuses.

In Union City, walking along Bergen Line Avenue, entering grocery stores and butcher shops, listening to the unchanging voice of my people in exile arguing about the price of meat and trips to Cuba, observing—absolutely stultified—the young living the lies of the old and delighting myself with the sway of the Cuban-American girls—whose walk verified the myth of the Caribbean women's derriere—I realized I seemed strange to them. I was nothing but a stranger, with my solitude and my heavy, painful, old load of history.

Animals are born without realizing it, by a process they don't understand; without beginning or end, without past or future, with the lone presence of their trails in the forest, their roads of air and sea. But, frozen in Union City, with thirty-three years of history that were centuries and at the same time only an instant, I couldn't find my way.

"Some people smile, but don't show their teeth." "Dogs are dogs." "Bad times follow good ones." "Better to walk alone than in bad company." "The darkest moment in the night is just before sunrise." "The one who pushes doesn't get hurt." "You never know who you're working for." "To die is the most natural thing." "The hat was so late coming, it didn't find a head." "If a rooster doesn't sing, it's because it has something in its throat." "The bigger the horse, the bigger the fall."

I don't know why the author insisted on my starting the story this way. I'll go along for now. I should then tell you that six months ago I was in Florida, burning rubber along the Sunshine State Parkway, challenging the Highway Patrol.

> Tenía que ser así
> Mi alma lo presintió
> Que cuando más te adoraba
> Te vas de mí ...

I left Miami in a hurry. The reason, if you need a reason, was her husband. Of course, there are other considerations, but I decided I had no desire to meet the man.

Te vas, yo no sé por qué,
La vida, la vida lo quiso así
Sabiendo cuánto te quiero
Te quieres ir ...

Consequently, I jumped through the bedroom window, something I had never done before. There was no reason to stay, and
the highway was nearby. It always seemed to be nearby when it
was imperative to skip town. Look at Butch Cassidy. In Montana
he took the highway and wound up in Patagonia. From Miami I
took the highway for New York and wound up in Havana.

At the time I had been enjoying the benefits of a literary fel-
lowship. I had six months before my work was done and I hadn't
committed a single word to paper. What can I do? It's always like
that; it's my fault, I know it. But why? Why should it be my fault?
Why should it be anyone's fault? Why should there be any fault
at all? The truth is I never finish anything. Shit, I must change.
The thing is that I like beginnings more than endings. Beginnings
nourish me. There is a nervous tension in starting something, an
innocence, like falling in love.

José Martí was a revolutionary and a poet. But the real fascination for me was the man himself; the man with his shortcomings
and his love affairs, with his drinking problem and his smoking
hash, with his hopes and his dreams. I could imagine him in his
puny room in New York planning, hoping, suffering. I wanted to
get to know that man of flesh and bones, as Unamuno would call
him, the man who carried a closed umbrella while it rained because
he considered it more beautiful that way.

In a country cursed by constant showers, like Cuba, it was always surprising to me as a child that I never saw a single soul
carrying an umbrella. At the first sign of rain everyone ran to the
nearest porch for protection.

"He took off like a rocket."

"He took off as if he'd been on fire."

"He took off as if there was no tomorrow."

"He took off without saying a word."

Had Martí not suffered as much for his people, he would have
become, without a doubt, the Don Juan of the New World. He
certainly had a way with words:

I thought of you and of your hair,
Envy of the shadow world.
Part of me I rested on them without care

Dreaming that you were my girl.

New York seemed like a good place to begin writing about
Martí; at least, that's what I kept telling myself as I drove across
Georgia.

Martí had lived in New York for almost fifteen years, longer
than any other place after leaving Cuba on his sixteenth birthday. He arrived on a cold, sunny afternoon in January, 1880. He
couldn't work in Spain. New York was closer to Cuba, closer to
the Revolution; and he had a spiritual necessity to be close to the
Revolution, whose leaders were men of action, military men; Martí
was an intellectual, and it was natural that friction would arise between them. But he was not about to let personal differences vitiate
the opportunity to liberate the island. He had already sacrificed
everything: his family life, his literary career, his health.

Yes, New York was the place for me. Who can write anything
serious in Florida, in 98 degree temperature? For my part, I must
confess I used to get up at sunset: anti-Floridian, I know.

"C'mon, boy, get out of the house."

"Go to the beach."

"Go and get some fresh air."

If and when I got up at mid-day, I would take a shower and put
on my white Pierre Cardin suit, St. Laurent silk shirt, and Bally
shoes. With this outfit, I would head for the Fontainbleau, or any
of the other dinosaur hotels of Miami Beach to sip frozen daiquiris.

I am born anywhere,
I walk and I don't have feet,
No one can see me,
Anyone will fight for me.
Who am I?
You give up?
I'm a lie.
Liberty was thus created.

2

The day I arrived in Miami, January 1st, 1959, the city had
been awakened by the cacophonous symphony of Cubans blowing
their automobile horns. They were celebrating the triumph of Castro's Revolution. The dormant vacation playland had never had
such commotion; the inhabitants, however, took it all in stride.
The Cubans wanted to go home! Good! They all concurred, giving a collective, Puritan nod of assent. At Miami International

Airport, the Cubans could be heard in what would turn out to be their short-lived euphoria, "If that is communism, I am a communist."

I was fourteen then. Growing up under the Florida sunshine, I was bound to a lifestyle that had ceased to exist, to a people I didn't really know, to a country with which I couldn't come to terms.

I left the boys my own age to enter the world of men and women some twenty years my senior. I became part of their passions, their joys and their sorrows, until six months ago. It was then that I felt myself out of place, out of step, out of time; I felt it like a shower on a sunny afternoon, like an omen you feel in your gut before it reaches your brain. I was on a one-way magical flight that would have to end in a spasm of conscience. Mine was a generation drifting among fading memories, uncertainties and a sense of not belonging. It was a generation wishing time would either stop in pre-Castro Cuba—1958—or, to the contrary, speed ahead full blast; wishing the Revolution had never taken place or, better still, that it would end tomorrow; wishing we were back in our homeland, in our hometowns, with our loved ones. We were exiles within an exile, having been caught in the middle: hearing the unchanging voices of our parents chanting songs of yesteryear; watching the boys and girls our age living the lies of the old; willing to give anything to have had a choice.

My newfound friends in Miami and I were a heterogeneous quintet: Mario Mar, his brother Lalo, Rolando Lima, Aldo and myself.

Mario Mar was a piano player and band leader. He played by ear, which forced him to rely on Ralph, the bass player, in order to get the band to play on tempo. Mario was short and stocky. I don't say fat, because he was quite sensitive about his weight; it wouldn't be an injustice, however, to say that food had gotten the best of him. Slender, piano players are not common in tropical orchestras for some reason. "Mario Mar and his Tropical Sound." Physically, he was rapidly deteriorating, although he had made up his mind not to let himself go. "I have my routine well laid out," he used to say, "every night, before going to bed, I put on a mask of egg whites." Pulling the soft, pink skin of his cheeks with the middle and index fingers of both hands, he would proudly display the results of his nightly treatments. "Look," he would announce with dreamy eyes, "like a baby's ass. I could sell Noxema on television." The yellowed index finger of his left hand was witness to the excessive smoking of the gregarious conversationalist and music maker. His indefatigable smile concealed the frustrations of an aging, lonely homosexual who had spent a lifetime pretending he was straight. His overweight frame gave the impression of a tired elephant who had lost its natural habitat. He was loving and wreckless; one couldn't help but love him.

Lalo, Mario's brother, besides being an amateur musician was also in the numbers racket. He had once been married, although he never spoke of his wife. His private life, he used to say, was his own business. Physically, he was Mario's antithesis: his skin was dark, he was wiry with a pronounced curvature of his back. What little hair he had was gray and curly. To make him angry all that was needed was to ask him the whereabouts of his grandmother (implying he had kinsmen who were black). His face became like concrete, his eyes bulged out of their sockets and his lips pushed one against the other as if they were football players on the one yard line. Saturday was his day of revelation; winners made a few dollars—which was proof enough of God's existence—while losers took the bad news philosophically, "Next week will be different." Lalo played the numbers, but his true love was the bongo drums. The bongos, also known in our slang as *timbales* were held between the knees, while keeping the legs crossed. But *timbales* was also a euphemism for testicles, so that when someone said, "*Tócame los timbales*," the person being addressed was never quite sure if he was being asked to play or to touch the other man's balls. The *bongos-timbales* were introduced to the New World when African rhythms began to be assimilated by the white musicians in their interpretation of the European country dance. This musical integration—the only integration allowed—gave birth to *La Contradanza*, the *Habanera*, and the *Rumba*. Lalo was a master bongo player; his great pursuit in life had become "making those goat skins sing." Though never as a professional, he satisfied his musical yearning by playing with Mario and myself in local bars on Saturday afternoons after the bets on the numbers had been paid. For this we received as payment all the free beer we could drink.

The third member was Rolando Lima, a frail, bespectacled sixty-year-old former policeman from Havana. A week after he began working at the Valencia grocery store, he became the manager, a feat that surprised even the owner. But most of his time was absorbed reminiscing about the good-old-days, when he was a police captain in Havana, in the late forties.

During those long, tropical nights when crime was slow in the Cuban capital, Rolando and some of his boys would cruise around town in a patrol car. On the Malecón, a wide street that runs along the promenade facing the bay and wraps itself around the city like a silk, blue ribbon, they usually ran into one of those sharply dressed dudes, *chucheros*, whose unusually wide pants had extremely narrow cuffs. Rolando would stop the *chuchero* and, speaking with a cigarette held tightly between his teeth, he would ask almost innocently, "Can you take off your pants without removing your shoes?" Right then and there the poor man had to prove he could do it. If he couldn't, they would beat him up.

The last member of our group was Aldo. His five-foot-ten inch frame couldn't contain the delight of his laughter. To face him was to be overwhelmed by his beady black eyes. When Castro came into power, Aldo was an architecture student at the University of Havana, where he had participated in student riots against Batista. In 1961, when he realized the new regime was turning too fast and too much to the left, he escaped by boat to Jamaica together with eight other students. Once in the United States, his desire to go back was so great that he had trouble settling down; he couldn't adapt; he couldn't learn the language—actually, he refused—he just couldn't see himself living permanently in the United States, so he didn't continue his university studies as his old schoolmates had. Instead, he married his childhood sweetheart. Between his family, his job and his anti-Castro activities, Aldo found enough time to chase after half the women in Miami, single or not. He had a contact: Luis Vega was a tall, heavyset homosexual from the Dominican Republic. On a Saturday afternoon, forfeiting my musical rendezvous with the Mars brothers, I joined Aldo on a visit to the exotic sexual treasure chest.

As I would later find, the door was always open. A palpable darkness, a penumbra from a Renaissance interior, a disturbing stillness. It took a few seconds before I was able to notice the maze of furniture in the living room. There was a bizarre, unearthly odor to the house; a mixture of smells, not chemical, nor culinary, nor floral. From the amalgam of scents I recognized basil, for it was used as an esoteric "cleansing" ritual performed by spiritualists. In my childhood, my mother realized that there was something wrong with my psychie or my soul, or both. I reluctantly was dragged to be treated by Panchelo, an old, black man with huge hands and feet. He would ask me to stand in the center of the living room, and close my eyes. Then, he would begin the ceremony by reciting some sort of prayer or litany in a foreign language. All of a sudden, there it was. The smell! Basil, sweet basil. As I was being transported to some celestial plateau, Panchelo began singing as he plunged the basil in a bucket full of cool water. I was in a total rapture, I heard angels sing, I saw the face of Nancy, the girl next door on whom I had a devastating crush, I felt a tickle down my spine, and it was then, as I floated in perfect ecstasy, that the wet bunch of basil leaves hit my face; I felt chills, I was trembling, I was afraid; but my mother had been reassured that I was her old, little, sweet boy once more, returned to her by the powerful hands of Panchelo and the mysteries of basil.

As we reached the dining room, I saw Luis close the door that led to the bedroom. He was wearing a short sleeve shirt and light blue slacks. His long legs took very short steps as he cooled his huge mass of soft flesh with a handheld cardboard fan, the kind they give away in drugstores. One side had an advertisement: "La Caridad Pharmacy." On the opposite side there was a colored illustration of the Sacred Heart, showing Christ with a serene, handsome face— more a blond Swedish sailor than a nomadic Jew—swaying to-and-fro with each movement of Luis's short, hairless left arm. Grabbing my outstretched hand with his chubby, baby-soft fingers, he gave me what I regarded as a passionate stare and proceeded to walk towards the backyard.

"Fate brought you to this house," he said without looking at me. "Oh, the mysteries of life." The sunlight hit my face like the flash of an impertinent photographer. The trees in the patio blocked out every trace of house and neighbor, even though they were but a few feet away. Mangos, oranges, lemons were accomplices to the fat man's fancies. There were several metal chairs and a table, all painted white. "Sit down," Luis said, as he slid—the Sacred Heart still swaying—into one of the chairs and filled the empty metal convexity as a turtle fits into its own shell.

"This is my garden," he continued, "where pleasure grows like these flowers, with all its sacred juices waiting in perfect compartments." The amicable, sensual, homosexual pimp paused for a moment, and looked around with complete delight, enjoying his teasing and the flow of his words which he thought impressed me. "You don't know it yet," he continued, "but you have a mission. You will refuse a fruit offered to you under the moon, under the branch of an unforgettable tree. You will meet strange beings and do strange things. It's all been laid out for you; you cannot fight it. Remember the number six. You will do good and bad things; you will be positive and negative at the same time; you will create and destroy. You carry the Seal of Solomon. You are fire and water. You are irreversibly attached to a god, a demi-god. You are a Virgo, aren't you?" He spoke with ease, relaxed as a Caribbean

Buddha who knew the mystery of the Bermuda Triangle and wasn't telling all he knew. "The fall is permitted," he continued, "in order that a greater good may come. We are only the instruments of a greater design: had there been no Fall, there would have been no need for Redemption."

I had no idea what the hell he was talking about; it didn't look to me as if he was trying to convert me to Christianity, but the Gospel according to Luis did not make an impression on me. He was the key to women and sex, so I followed the initiation with all the innocence I could muster, trying to hold on to a straight face while, from the corner of my eye, I could see Aldo, who was in stitches.

3

Miami, Miami, Miami, oh, my! Tampa and Key West had been, for over a century, home away from home for Cubans opposed to the government on the island; but in the high-tech-exile from Castro's Revolution, it was Miami, blessed with sunshine, white sandy beaches, hurricanes, art deco and republicans that opened its reluctant arms (as a willing but confused virgin) to the half million, fun-loving, hard-working *rumba* dancers.

Miami was a city that swayed to Lawrence Welk, but the *mambo* and the *cha-cha* (I can't explain why Americans dropped the third *cha* in *cha-cha-cha*: it was either laziness or lack of rhythm) would soon reign. The most predominant billboard, that of a cute blond girl smiling as she looked over her shoulder, proudly showing off the pink skin of her untanned bottom from beneath her bikini, would soon give way to the sensuous smile of a latin beauty holding a glass of beer in her hand with long, perfect red nails: PARA CUANDO TENGA DESEOS DE TOMAR MAS DE UNA, the suggestive copy would read with its obvious double entendre. Oh, Miami! Let me sing of thy virtues and thy Bermuda shorts; let me praise thy architecture (circa 1959) of small, wooden, white-painted little structures, otherwise called houses; let me praise thy huge motorcycle policemen who, in my twelve-year-old boy fantasies, were knights in starched white shirts and dark glasses. Oh, my Miami! Anguished masturbation double features of exposed flesh in the glorious Olympia Theatre with its domed ceiling painted in a distinct ultramarine blue, with bright stars dancing to-and-fro; Miami encounters with voluptuous prostitutes—more about that later—; streets of Miami that I walked on Sunday afternoons, the only free afternoons I had between school and the

El Paso Supermarket, where I worked as a stock boy since I was thirteen. On those Sunday afternoons, I would wear my best dark blue slacks and continental (I thought) print shirt to go walking past the houses of girls I wanted to impress, while holding a large book in my right hand (intellect was always a fetish of mine). Miami quartered by Flagler Street and Miami Avenue.

In the Miami school that I attended I was unable to understand a word of English. I went from class to class at the sound of each bell, as a member of a ballet from a foreign opera. Miami, where I was a *spic* when I didn't even know the meaning of the word; Miami Senior High School, where I learned to eat meatloaf with peas and carrots, where I slept in history class along with the teacher (the fact that the class was right after lunch may have had something to do with our inability to stay awake). "Tepee, canoe and Tyler to ... " the overweight, balding teacher holding a four-foot stick in his hand would doze off, and being the good student I was, I followed while the sun beat on us with all its fury through the high-opened windows. Miami sports that I couldn't play, because I had to work, and later I was forced to say, as Brando said: "I could have been a contender." I had the body, the physical abilities; I could have been the first Cuban quarterback (Is such a thing possible?). Miami Veronica, my first American girlfriend: short, with curly black hair and a big nose, but I didn't care, " 'cause American girls went all the way." You didn't have to romance them like Latin girls. Miami, my initiation into the pornography of poetry: bastardizations that we made at lunchtime of famous verses using foul language; my first burst of creativity in English. Miami, how I loved thee then, when the world was small and I learned about life as I grew up along thy streets and thy girls' thighs.

4

One day Aldo, a man whose friendship I treasure to this day, gave me the greatest gift a man can bestow on a friend: her name was Rosario, a lively forty-year-old former beauty queen with a gargantuan smile. During her prolonged and persistent laughter, her round, full, red lips created an abyss that was an invitation to a suicidal leap of pleasure.

I spotted her leaving the supermarket carrying a large bag of groceries; I offered to help. She lived on the ground floor of a dilapidated three-story apartment building. We entered through the kitchen door. I placed the bag of groceries on a blue formica dinette table with orange flowers in large and small spirals. She offered to make coffee and I accepted.

As she filled the coffee maker while talking over her left shoulder, she was a delight to Ruben's eyes; a mountainous landscape of firm flesh; an erotic maze to get lost in. I struck a match and got the pilot going. As she placed the pot on the fire, we were almost touching. A strange, exotic smell emanated from her body. It excited me. An amber glow filled the room. The walls and ceiling were finished in careless stucco painted in a light peach color.

"You're very popular," she said with a wicked smile, "all the little girls in the neighborhood are crazy about you."

I didn't answer. Pretending to hide my pride, I smiled as if I had not taken her statement seriously. She was tempting, almost beautiful in an earthy way.

"I had wanted to talk to you for the longest time," I said, "but I couldn't bring myself to do it; I didn't know how to approach you."

I was bullshitting her, and she played along. She wanted to hear my praise of her beauty, which she knew had passed, but she pretended it hadn't, and she simply looked at me with her big eyes, wanting to hear more.

"You should have," she said, and I felt her words bouncing inside my mouth.

What followed was a desperate attempt to get rid of the minimal amount of clothes to allow us to bring to a resolution what we both knew was inevitable. The flowery dinette table began to rattle; the bag of groceries fell to the ground; the dozen eggs which were on top created an expressionistic landscape on the kitchen floor; a tomato rolled until it came to rest at the foot of the refrigerator; the coffee, which had been boiling, began to overflow, forming a burnt umber lake on the stove; the landscape of eggs reached my brightly polished loafers; our passion was gaining the momentum of a roller coaster on its way down, as a sprinter on the last ten yards; my eyes were staring at the peachy stucco; her fingernails were already making their way into my shoulders, and then: A Chinese New Year; I heard an "Oh, God," that had the makings of a television evangelist, but I replied with an equally deafening, "Oh, Rosario."

Rosario had left Cuba in 1965 with her two-year-old boy; her husband stayed behind. He gave her up for the Revolution, and a female revolutionary. She couldn't put up with either of them, so she decided to start anew. Without a husband, without money, with a small boy and a demented look on her face, she left the island in a twelve-foot boat together with seven or eight other people.

Her only contact in the United States was a distant cousin on her mother's side who lived in New York. After being rescued by the American Coast Guard while still quite far from Key West, the hungry, thirsty, sunburnt group, with Rosario's boy screaming and clinging to his mother's breasts, were taken to Miami. She gave the authorities the name and telephone number of her cousin in New York; he would serve as her sponsor. Mario, Rosario's cousin, worked in an Italian restaurant in Queens. As soon as she arrived in Jackson Heights, he got her a job at the restaurant, acting in a Christmas sketch, which the native Neapolitans presented every year from December 15th to the 6th of January. She had done some acting in Havana, before she got married. Actually, she had done some television commercials—not because of her acting abilities, but because of the director's fascination with her derriere.

In an Italian restaurant in New York, Rosario began her new life as the Virgin Mary six nights a week and twice on Sundays, while her small boy stayed at home with a neighbor.

"Isn't this country something?" she enjoyed exclaiming. "After two husbands, an abortion and a child, I've gone back to being a virgin. This must be the American dream."

After the Christmas season, she began working in a glove factory in lower Manhattan, but she had troubles making ends meet. The cold began to take its toll on the former tropical beauty, but it was the city's somber solitude, the lack of human contact, of friendly greetings that were her worst adversaries. Finally, they got the best of her. She left New York for Miami, where she hoped the soothing tropical breezes would come to her rescue. One day a neighbor of her's who was known as "La China," even though she was not Chinese, invited Rosario to go out with two male companions. It all sounded innocent enough, and she hadn't danced since the old days in Havana. The evening proved to be fun, embarrassing, profitable and shameful: it was the beginning of a life she had never expected to lead.

5

The sun was particularly grueling that Saturday afternoon as I stood on the corner of North West 7th Street and 23rd Court. I wasn't looking at anything in particular, nor was I going anywhere. I was just standing there, perspiring, while I watched Lalo and the chemist from the drugstore down the street bet on license plates as the cars rushed by. I was lost. I had no friends my age; my family didn't know who I really was. I still lived at home, but we were strangers. We had nothing to share, nothing to say. It was all silent love; no feelings were ever expressed; not a word said, not an embrace given.

I was surviving Miami's heat, mumbling to myself an old Cuban song, one that I remembered from my childhood, that I had learned from the radio or from hearing it blasting through the open door of a dark smelly bar. My closest link to my country, to my culture, to my childhood and to myself was music, sensuous music, intoxicating music, music that makes you move even through your reluctance. I was a product of the *son*, of the *bolero* and the *rumba*. I was a syncopated man, living the musical notation of swaying hips and perspiring breasts. I was misplaced among the misplaced; exiles lost in a Floridian desert of remembrances; nourishment made of memories, days lived from stories retold ad infinitum, from eating ad infinitum the food of our ancestors, believing the beliefs we didn't believe but were part of our tradition, of our so called culture, our daily bread, our daily looking at the mirror before shaving.

Rolando Lima came by, and told me that two of his lieutenants from the Havana police, who now had an export-import business in Miami, needed someone to take a shipment of dishwashers to Honduras; since he knew I needed money, Rolando had volunteered me for the Central American venture. I had always heard that Tegucigalpa, the capital of Honduras was the asshole of the world. Being a good Freudian, I jumped at the occasion.

6

To arrive in Honduras from the United States is to have your senses awaken from a lethargic existence: colors, sounds, smells; it's like experimenting everything for the first time. We made our approach over the Comayagua mountains. As a hungry falcon over a defensive prey, our plane took a dive, coming dangerously close to a dusty road whose only sign of live was a poor peasant family making its way on their knees and nothing more than blind faith to the sanctuary of the Virgin of Suyapa.

The Hotel Honduras Maya, in the best Hilton tradition, offered swimming pool, Tom Collins and smiling faces. It would serve as our hideout, our rendezvous point, our oasis of intrigues, romance and clean sheets. Late in the afternoon, standing on the terrace that overlooked the city, the somber, gray face of the capital looked like the end of the world from our concrete and glass mountain. Iguanas and bananas dominated the local diet of the people who wore easy smiles on sad faces, and whose worn blue jeans hid their skinny, dark legs. The first thing that moved me was the people's tenderness, kept alive at all costs in the hope that it would not betray the hunger and poverty in their lives. How I suffered with Tegucigalpans on that fading American afternoon! America in the larger sense of the world; the larger America, that old-by-now New World; the America of Bolívar and Martí, who knew so well the danger of being a neighbor to the United States: "I have lived in the heart of the monster, and I know it well."

"It's not bad here, is it?" a chubby, gray-haired man said as he glanced at me with a smile.

"It's my first time," I answered. "I never imagined it like this, but you're right, it's not bad here."

"Where do you come from?"

"I'm Cuban."

"I have lots of friends in Cuba," he said with pride in his voice. "Ramiro Valdez is a good friend of mine. I just saw him a couple of months ago in Havana. Did you just arrive?"

"I'm just passing by."

"Fernando Viera," he announced, extending me his hand, "I'm the secretary of the Communist Party here."

"Miguel Saavedra," I said shaking hands.

"This country is in shambles, just look around: poverty everywhere. There are neighborhoods we can't see from here, where the rich, the politicians and the military live. Their children study in the United States; they go shopping in Miami. But things are going to change; it's already started. Not only here, all over Central America: Nicaragua, El Salvador, whether they want it or not. Right here, in this hotel, you go to the bar or to the restaurant, and you'll hear the Americans, all government agents, making plans for Honduras as if this was Oklahoma or California; they don't give up. That's because they're in the forest and they don't see the trees. In their own country they're more liberal than anyone, but they don't want anyone else in the rest of the world to be liberal; they want all the liberties for their citizens, but the rest of the world should be controlled by a petty dictator whom they can control; they prosper and we suffer. You know what I'm talking about. We're going to take their Honduran candy from them. We're learning from you Cubans. You have given us strength."

I observed that the sexagenarian, despite his rhetoric, was quite likable with his long, wavy hair and his funny accent. I couldn't help but think that I had just arrived in an incongruous world of inequalities, frustrations and even hope. That was the real America, the America I didn't know, the lost America, an America that from afar looked deformed, an America of extremes, the other America, our America. The old Honduran dreamer actually thought that I had just come from Cuba, not from Miami; he thought that I was a member of Castro's government; he thought I was one of them. What else would I be doing there? Even though I didn't just arrive from Cuba, even though I wasn't a member of the Cuban government, I was one of them: a romantic, an optimist in an imaginary America without frontiers, an Ariel or Caliban? These two literary characters marked the great dilemma of our culture.

"There was only stillness and silence in the darkness of the night," said the old man. "Only the Creator, the Giver of Form, Tepen, Gueumatz, the progenitors were in the water, surrounded by water. They hid behind green and blue feathers, that is why they are called Gueumatz. Thus was the existence of heaven, and the heart of heaven also, which is the nave of God, how He is called.

"Then, when word arrived, Tepen and Gueumatz came together in the dark of night, they spoke among themselves and meditated; they put their words and their thoughts together.

"It became clear, as they meditated, that at daybreak man should appear. And they ordered the creation and the growing of the trees and the bindweeds and the birth of life and the creation of man ...

"Do you see that river over there?" The amicable communist asked, while pointing into the distance. "That is the Big River. It's not much of a river, as you can see. The only thing that flows in it is a mist, a dampness, a faint memory of water which used to come down from the mountains. If you look close enough, you will see men squatting carelessly to relieve themselves; you will see women who come to the river to wash themselves, still dressed, in the light of day.

"Once the creation of the quadrupeds and the birds was finished, it was said to them by the Creator, the Giver of Form and the progenitors: Speak, shout, chirp, call out, speak, each one according to its species. This was said to the deer, the birds, the lions, the tigers and the serpents.

"Then, say our name. Invoke the hurricane, Chipi, Caculha, Raxa-Caculha, the Heart of Heaven, the Heart of the Earth, the Creator, the Giver of Form, the progenitors; speak, call to us, worship us! So they were told.

"But, nothing succeeded in making man speak; the humans shrieked, cackled and croaked, but no pattern of language manifested itself; each individual gave his particular cry ...

"Poverty here has reached drastic proportions," the old man said. "It has reached a new dimension. People in Paris or New York cannot imagine this, but in spite of it all, these people are alive, they have passion, they have hope. Damn it! There is life here.

"So it was that the Creator, the Giver of Form and the progenitors had to try once more to create man.

"Let's try again! Dawn approaches; lets make the one who will support and nourish us! How else will we be invoked and remembered?

"Look, I don't believe in God," the old man continued, "but for the believers Central America must be a great punishment; most likely not enough 'Our Fathers' were said to meet the requirements. So this is what they got, a miserable concoction of hunger and dictators.

"Then, the creation and formation of man took place. From soil, from mud, flesh was made. But they saw it didn't work, the body melted, it was soft, it didn't have movement nor strength, it fell down, it was watery, its head didn't move, the face would go sideways, its sight was veiled, it couldn't see backwards. At the beginning it spoke, but it could not understand. In no time water over-powered it, and it could not sustain itself ...

"Hunger makes you weak," he said softly, "not only physically, but your morale as well. Who can afford to have principles on an empty stomach? This country has to turn communist.

"Immediately, they destroyed their work and their creation, and said, 'What shall we do to correct it, so that our worshipers come out perfect?'

"The next thing was the divination, the drawing of lots with the corn and the Tzite. Luck! Creature!

"Then they spoke the truth: our dolls will do well if they are made of wood; they will speak and they will endure on the face of the earth.

"We're ready to give it all we've got," he continued; "more likely than not, the whole country will never be as rich as a single American corporation, but at least, we would not have to see another child die of hunger.

"The poet Luis Cardoza y Aragon told us that 'the Supreme Creator gave us the corn; he sprinkled the grains all over, on the cold mountain and the hot plains as a blessing. The Mayan boy's bellybutton was cut with an obsidian knife. The blood was spread on the cob, then the grains were sowed until the boy could do it by himself; his life then would be long and fruitful.' Our soil and our bellies were filled with corn, we lived with it, we grew up with it. Now it's time for us to stop living from corn, just as we must stop living under the shadow of the American corporations. Our nourishment from now on should no longer be corn, but Marxism. What do you think?"

I didn't answer; instead I stood up and let my eyes wander along the gray Tegucigalpa panorama. This poor, dirty, miserable country was what kept the old man alive; it gave him a reason to live, to fight. It was something I didn't have. I saw then that not only didn't I have a country to care for, but I really had no one to care for. The old man continued to speak, but I couldn't make out his words. The brown sky fell on the city like a deep suntan. I turned to the old man, shook his hand and said goodbye. "Come to see me before you leave," he said, "I want to send a few things to Cuba."

By ten o'clock, wearing a suit and tie, I was on my way to the Presidential Palace for a gala reception. As I passed skinny Honduran soldiers wearing old American army uniforms, it came to me that I had been living, but not wanting to remember; I was always on the outside, indifferent, apathetic. I had lived without details, hiding important facts; I had passed by unnoticed; my life had been one of caprice and fear, of melancholy and love for a few friends who were exiles from a life and a place I never knew, but that somehow I longed for.

As I entered the Presidential Palace, the glitter of chandeliers, silver, lights, bright uniforms, extravagant gowns and plastic civility made me think of my communist friend of the afternoon. There was no poverty here, no hunger, no sad faces. On that day I had seen four hundred years of Latin American history pass in front of my eyes.

I didn't know anyone, nor did anyone come to greet me. Making my way through the crowded room I reached the President-General-Dictator-Smiling Soldier who stood in the middle of a hall the size of a football field.

"Miguel Saavedra," I said, outstretching my hand.

"Welcome," said the smiling soldier in olive green perfection. "You are not Honduran."

"Cuban," I said.

"Cuban? But, from this side, no?"

"Yes, Miami."

"No wonder. Otherwise you wouldn't be here. I got some of your compatriots from the other side here in the mountains. Tomorrow I'm driving up there to take care of the problem, even though I got a hernia. You want to come? You're welcome to come and beat the shit out of them."

All of a sudden, I noticed a photographer taking my picture, as two other men approached us at full speed. They had just realized that a total stranger had penetrated their ranks and was alone with the general.

"He's one of us," the general said to his bodyguards, as he wrapped me in his decorations, olive green with golden fringe. "At five in the morning, we'll be on our way; I will send a jeep for you. You're at the Honduras Maya, right? We'll have fun tomorrow hunting down Cubans. Get a good night's sleep."

He was laughing out loud as he walked away, leaving me as the center of attention. Not knowing what to do next, I began to sing.

7

I was sitting at my typewriter when I made up this story; but maybe that's not what I was really doing, maybe I was just writing it. It was or could have been true, like everything else in life; it all depends on how you look at it. It didn't simply flow crisp and clear as the timid jet of water from the little, wrinkled penis of a marble cherub. Instead, it came and went capriciously as a hose out of control on a passive lawn. It didn't really concern me if I did or did not have the right to tell it. I had tried to stay close to the facts; no one had to remind me that fiction had no obligation to tell the truth. But somehow, the fantasy in our stories or the stories in our fantasies will always go hand in hand. Writers are not what Stalin called them, "Engineers of the soul," a name he called them when he shipped them out to Siberia to preserve their engineering: the individual is nothing, the system is everything. The novel can be art or entertainment, social commentary or political act, it's a training camp for the imagination. You are what you read, but you are also what you write. I was part of this story, even though it's not autobiographical. I wrote it on my Smith-Corona. How would non-Latin Americans react to this story? After all, we aren't just Carmen Miranda, Ricky Ricardo, bananas, tangos and tacos. For hundreds of years we were the New World, the second one after the Old; all of a sudden we have become the Third World. Who knows what other worlds are in store for us.

On Sunday, June 8th, 1969, in this football stadium in Tegucigalpa, the national teams of Honduras and El Salvador met in a classifying game, to see who would advance to the World Cup in Mexico the following year.

The team from El Salvador arrived the day before the big game, in order to get a good night's rest and to acclimate themselves to the host city. Tegucigalpa turned out to not be only the host, but also the hostile city. The Salvadoran players weren't able to get as much as a minutes sleep on that fateful eve; the fans of the host team had the hotel under siege, bombarding the old colonial structure with bricks and stones, while others banged steel drums and zinc plate with wooden sticks; dozens of cars blew their horns incessantly; firecrackers went off religiously every five minutes. The Honduran reception had as a finale a boisterous serenade of obscene songs.

Sunday's game was played as scheduled, but the tired, sleepy, nervous and angry team from El Salvador as could be expected, lost the game during the last minute of play. Meanwhile, in San Salvador, a teenaged girl who had been watching the game on television jumped out of her chair and ran to the study, where her father usually kept his gun. She opened the drawer, took the pistol, and without a moment's hesitation, shot herself through the heart. The following morning, the newspaper *El Nacional*, reporting the suicide of the football fan, said that the poor girl could not bear to see her country fall to its knees. The sad story of the teenager shook the nation; there was mourning throughout the country, in all the cities and villages, in the countryside, in government circles, in the homes of both rich and poor. Her death was a national tragedy, which manifested itself at her burial. An army honor guard headed the procession; even the President attended, together with all his ministers, who walked, with bowed heads, behind the casket covered with the Salvadoran flag. At the tail end of the procession came the eleven football players with tears in their eyes.

The following week the second game took place in the Flor Blanca Stadium, in San Salvador. This would prove to be Salvador's revenge. On the eve of the game, Salvadoran fans outdid their Honduran counterparts in harassment and insults. After a sleepless night and a barrage of rotten eggs, dead rats and stones which left no window untouched, the Honduran players had to be escorted to the playing field by a division of army soldiers. The stadium was cordonned off with a regiment of the National Guard. Needless to say, the scared Hondureans didn't have a prayer that day, on or off the field. Protected by the machine guns of the army, the players made it safely to the airport; their fans, however, weren't so lucky. The faithful who had traveled to their adversarys' lair to give their team moral support were punched, kicked and clubbed; they left two dead and dozens injured. Enough was enough; football could no longer settle the matter: the time for war had arrived.

Our greatest ideology is that of the fatherland; rich and poor, religious and non-believers, artists and soldiers all become a single entity when it comes to defending the national dignity.

The little war lasted one hundred hours, after which six thousand lay dead, twelve thousand wounded, and fifty thousand homeless. I pondered all this as I sat in my apartment and told that story without the consent of the government or the militia as one must have in Rumania, where first and last name must be given, together with that of the parents, the place in which one works, the number and model of the typewriter, explaining how one came about it and for what purpose it was being used. If and when one's application was approved, one would receive notification—some two months later—authorizing the use of the typewriter; however not before the alleged writer brought the typing machine in question to the local office of the militia, on a given date, so that a sample of the type could be taken, sort of a typewriter fingerprint or blood test. The entire process must be repeated the first two months of the year, for each year that the writing object is in one's possession. Of course, I didn't live in Rumania, but I couldn't rightly say that I have anyone's blessing for writing these things of "Our America."

8

At four in the morning, the President-General came calling. We left my hotel leading an army convoy and headed for the brown mountains to the north. I was given an American-made M-16A1, as the General burst into laughter, "Let's hunt Cubans!" When the sun gave birth to a new day, the brown of the mountains gave way to deep greens. We were on foot, following orders transmitted by radio. The skinny, dark soldiers in American army fatigues didn't look to me like fire-eating green berets. The President-General walked ahead, holding his testicles on and off, and I followed him in my bright Hawaiian shirt and New York Yankee baseball cap ruffled in hand, and a dubious look on my face, concerned as I was with the General's Cuban hunting expedition. I began lighting a cigar, when two M-48 Patton II tanks open fired. Soldiers took their positions; M-203 grenade launchers went off all around me; the President-General laughed, displaying his bright, gold-filled teeth and shouting, "Sons-of-bitches, come out, I got a little present for you!" A plane flew over us and dropped a couple of bombs in the distance, but not far enough away for my liking. The President-General continued showing off his teeth and

holding his balls. "Here they come, here they come!" someone
cried out. Indeed, they were not only coming, but firing as well.
"Get'm, Cubano, get'm," I heard the President-General shouting
at me. One of the little soldiers to my right was hit, and his blood
became part of the free-flowing pattern of my Hawaiian shirt. I
had never shot anyone before in my life, but somehow I open fired
with my M-16. The plane continued bombing, the tanks advanc-
ing, the President-General laughing, the little soldiers falling, the
Cubans coming, and I kept on firing.

I don't know how the hell I let myself be talked into selling dish-
washing machines to Hondurans; I don't know why in the world I
was firing at Cubans, my compatriots; I don't know why the hell I
was the only one wearing a bright red Hawaiian shirt in the mist
of those emerald green mountains. Fuck it, Miguel Saavedra, get
the hell out of there! General, son-of-a-bitch, you and your fucking
hernia, let go of your balls and let's get out of here! Daydreaming had nothing to do with our Cuban hunting expedition; it was
kill or be killed. I can't say I killed anyone, but I certainly fired
quite a few rounds. By ten in the morning, it was all over. The
President-General smiled at me and said, "Damn it, Cubano, we
did it, hernia and all, hell. Let's get us some pussy."

We got in our jeep and began our drive back to town, while the
wounded soldiers were being attended to. The President-General,
two little soldiers and myself stopped at a bar on the outskirts
of the dirt town that we had passed on the way to our hunt. As
we entered, the President-General, imagining he was a Honduran
Marcus Ulpius Trajanus, grabbed one of the teenaged girls who had
been waiting at a table. They looked sad and sick, with their cheap
dresses, badly painted lips and dirty feet. "Pick one, Cubano," the
President-General said, "we have to celebrate." I couldn't pick
one, I couldn't celebrate. But a girl came to me anyway. She must
have been thirteen or fourteen. She took me by the hand and led
me into a dark, dirty little room that smelled of cold beer, piss,
semen and vomit. I sat on the bed and the girl began to undress.
"Don't do that," I said, but by that time she was naked, standing
in front of me. A faint ray of light came through the worn out
curtains. All I saw was the ad in *The New York Times*, appealing
to the American sense of decency, to adopt a child in the Third
World. Was she begging me to adopt her, I thought, to make love
to her, to spank her, to send her home, to call her parents, to get
her drunk?

"The General will pay," she said timidly.

"Yes, I know the General will pay," I said as I left the room. I got into the jeep and drove off.

9

Mario Mar and I went to pick up Lalo, who was having lunch with Roberto Lima at a restaurant nearby. It was Saturday, and we were getting ready for our musical afternoon. As we entered the restaurant, Roberto Lima was holding court:

"Imagine the year 1492 an hour before sunrise, on Friday, August 3rd. Three Spanish ships have just left the seaport of Palos under the leadership of an Italian named Cristoforo. On October 28th, they reached an island of which he said: 'It's the fairest island human eyes have yet beheld.' He had no idea where the hell they were. This must be Catayo, he thought, belonging to the Grand Khan; but as luck would have it, the poor bastard had only made it to Cuba: thus, we started our history on the wrong foot.

"The Spaniards kept on coming, followed by the British, who in turn were followed by the Americans: everyone wanted a piece of the sugar-cane pie.

"The natives that Columbus found didn't last long; they died from overwork and starvation. Someone came up with the idea of starting slave trade with Africa. When it got to the point that blacks were not enough to help the Spaniards ransack the little island, they began importing Chinese. The blacks were smart; they said, 'Fuck these Spanish people,' and turned to their old African religion for support, transforming their deities into the images of Catholic saints. In time, however, more white people were converted to the African religion than blacks into Catholicism. The Chinese couldn't hack it, though, they couldn't stand slavery. They would hang themselves the first chance they got or commit mass suicide. By 1868, the natives—dressed in their newborn nationalism—had enough and decided to rebel against the foreign oppressors. For ten years they fought, but nothing came of it. In 1895, they revolted once again; this time they were going all out. What do you think happened next? The Americans got into the picture! Remember the Maine? Well, that did it. The Spanish-American War came and went, and the Cubans, who had been fighting for over thirty years, were told to fuck off. This did nothing for our national morale. In 1902, the Republic was born—with a puppet Cuban-American president selected by you-know-who—but only frustration and disgrace followed. Then, Castro, the Revolution, exile.

"We're in Miami now, the Cuban exile capital of the world, the new Cuba; here we smoke cigars, drink black coffee, send

medicines to Cuba, curse Castro, build beautiful homes and reminisce about the past. On occasion, we drink the famed rum and
Coke with a twist of lime; it used to be called *Cuba Libre*, 'Free
Cuba.' However, here people know it isn't true, so they call it *una
mentirita*, a little lie. After all, this is Little Havana."

"There is a woman in my building," Lalo said, "who just went
back to Cuba to see her mother, she was dying or something. Anyway, this woman had never been back since she came in '59. Well,
when she came back, everyone was eager to know what was going
on in Cuba, I mean, firsthand, a direct report from someone they
knew, so they all flocked to the woman's apartment to hear about
her experience. Was it true that there was nothing to eat? Were
there still as many political prisoners? What was the mood of the
people? The woman, who was weary from the emotionally drain-
ing experience, sat in the center of her living room facing the eager
crowd. 'I tell you,' she began after taking a deep breath, barely
holding back her tears, 'I couldn't believe it, it's so hot, and the
flies!' 'Flies?' the crowd responded in unison. With their mouths
open they awaited to have their curiosity satisfied. 'No, no, no'
she obliged, 'I don't care what they tell me, there were never that
many flies in Cuba before the Revolution.'"

"Those are Cubans for you," Mario Mar exclaimed as we sat
down. "Give me a beer, beautiful," he said to the middle-aged
waitress, with hair teased into a spiral like a primitive rocket. "Another one for my friends here, he has to sing some good *boleros* in
an hour."

"The worst thing Castro did," said a fat, white-haired man who
was eating swordfish with white rice and green plantains, "was that
he stopped the democratic process."

Lalo took a sip from his beer and asked, "What democratic
process?"

"Elections," exclaimed Rolando Lima. "He stopped the elec-
toral process, our ability to elect the president we wanted."

"They were all crooks," Lalo answered back.

"Wait a minute," said the little man eating swordfish, "we've
had good presidents."

Mario Mar, who was apolitical, but who enjoyed a good laugh
asked, "Name one."

Roberto Lima picked up the old man's argument and interjected, "Prio was the best president Cuba ever had."

"What the hell are you talking about," Lalo said, "Carlos Prio,
besides being a gangster, was a thief. He became a multimillionaire
in four years."

Mario Mar, who was enjoying the tropical platonic dialogue to the hilt, continued to add fuel to the fire, "I think Grau was the best president we ever had."

Ramon Grau San Martin, I must explain to my uninitiated readers, was a tall, sick looking, ugly, pale, and by Cuban standards, effeminate professor of physiology at the University of Havana. He was a society doctor who incongruously also belonged to the underground opposition during the government of Gerardo Machado, the former General during the War of Independence against Spain—a.k.a. the Spanish-American War—who was elected president of the young republic in 1925; by 1930, he realized he enjoyed stealing from the people so much that he bribed Congress into changing the Constitution so that he could remain in power. His great achievement was building a highway down the center of the island, with the help of some hefty American loans: a thousand feet of road is a thousand dollars for me, Machado said to himself. This accounts for the extraordinary length of the highway. Returning to Grau, however, in 1933 he became provisional president of Cuba for one hundred and twenty days, when a dark-skinned, Chinese-looking sergeant named Fulgencio Batista put an end to the tall doctor's political prescription.

A lady sitting next to the white-haired man intervened, "I think the best president we ever had was Machado."

"Machado!" the woman exclaimed, gagging on the roast pork the woman was eating midway down her esophagus.

"Chase Manhattan, my good woman," Mario Mar exclaimed philosophically.

"Sweetie, give me a coffee," Lalo said.

"They were all crooks," Mario Mar continued.

"Any one of them was better than Fidel," Roberto Lima interjected.

"You can say that again," the woman said.

"I don't know about that," said Mario Mar.

"You are communist?" the old man asked.

"I'm a free spirit," my fat pianist continued.

"You're a communist," the woman exclaimed, pushing away her plate of roast pork.

"That's like saying that the black beans I had yesterday were better than the rice and chicken I had today."

"What are you talking about?" "Listen, I've been to the Dominican Republic." "Who cares." "I've been to Peru, to a little village where it never rains." "I've just arrived from Santo Domingo and it hasn't rained there, what do you say to that?" "The thing is

that you tell people here, and no one believes you." "The Dominican Republic is just like Cuba, the fruits are the same." "They
have real flavor, not like these things you eat here." "The same
thing in that village in Peru I was telling you about, even though
it never rains." "Here in Miami they're planting all the tropical
fruits." "Yeah, but they don't have the same taste."

10

I was returning home after our gig in the bar of a Miami Beach
hotel when I met Rosario. I was still feeling the aftereffects from
my Honduran adventure and the many beers I just had; I didn't
know if that had anything to do with it, but I think I was just
seeing her for the first time, the way she really was, I mean; she
looked very old and beat-up to me. She asked me to her house.
Not knowing how to say no, I went along. This time we entered
through the living room. Against a wall there was a couch covered
in blue brocade; in front of it, near a window, was an armchair
done in amethyst-colored crushed velvet. A low, formica coffee
table was in front of the couch; on top of it, a crystal vase with
plastic yellow roses and red gladiolus dominated the decor.

Rosario began to take off her flower-print jersey dress, and proceeded to throw her clothes on the armchair. Almost whispering
she said, "Don't make too much noise, my son is sleeping in the
next room." This caught me off guard. I didn't know what to
say. She was wearing old-fashioned bloomers, the kind I remember older women in Cuba wearing. Rosario looked at me invitingly,
biddingly, with sad eyes.

"Aren't you taking off your clothes?" she asked. I couldn't. I
felt ridiculous in front of the aging prostitute who was trying to
find love—or at least comfort—in a young, displaced writer who
had no love to give. We both stood still, silently facing each other,
not knowing what to say next. "It's all right," she said. "He never
wakes up."

"I think we better not," I said.

"It's all right, really," she insisted.

As tenderly as I could, I said, "Some other time, okay?" I
turned around, opened the door and walked into the dark and
carelessly kept hallway, illuminated by a single twenty-five watt
bulb over the main entrance. As I headed home, all I could see
was Rosario, naked, except for her large bloomers and sad smile.

11

I wasn't in a partying mood when Aldo came to pick me up. I went anyway just to satisfy an old friend of love and war. When I last saw Mario Mar he didn't look well; I had been calling him for the past couple of days without success; not even his brother knew of Mario's whereabouts. I attended the party full of reservations. What I never expected, though, was that Aldo and I were the only men invited; the other guests were six women, a perfect picture of Baudelaire's *Luxe, Calme et Volupte*: respectfully married to prominent men in the seaside community. Luis, a sexual Machiavelian, had arranged a weekend fishing trip for all their husbands. The first thing I noticed was the music. Roberto Ledesma, a Cuban-born, Frank Sinatra-style singer, was flooding the record player. A circus of over-dramatized furniture had been piled against the walls as if awaiting the hand of an interior decorator, while a lone lamp was burdened with the thankless job of creating a romantic atmosphere. The six middle-aged graces danced naked in the dark like a stream of unending pleasure. Partners changed, positions changed. Thighs, pubic hair, breasts and lips all mingled into one. Laughter and sighs, breaths and moans crisscrossed each other like zephyrs. Scolding whispers and wings of orgasms flew all over the room.

Around two in the morning, I staggered out of the house and drove over to the Police Benevolent Association—the PBA held latin dances every weekend at their headquarters—where Mario Mar was playing with his "typical orchestra." I was making my way through the perspiring mass of dancers; the music was intense, loud, intoxicating; I caught a glimpse of Mario at the piano; he was pale, his eyes were closed; all of a sudden he hit a dissonant chord, fell forward and banged the upright piano with his head. Pushing dancers left and right, I made it to the stage. He was dead. I didn't hear the music stop, nor the people who were screaming. I was frozen in an interminable loneliness. The police who were in the patio rushed in. An ambulance was called, the body was taken away, the dance ended, the smiles died away, the dancers went home.

I had been living in Miami for twenty years; like a flash, they passed in front of my eyes as I held Mario's body in my arms. Somehow I got home. The green of the trees had given way to black patches that covered most of the houses. The whole city was silent; the coffee shop across the street had already closed; its red and green neon sign was finally at rest for the night; the next day it would light up again, shouting its Cafe Cubano all over Flagler Street. I went out to the terrace, facing north and stared into the distance. I remembered that when I was a boy in Cuba, everytime someone was in trouble—financial or political—north was the only place to go. Following an old tropical tradition, I crammed my books and clothes into my '71 Chevy and drove off. By mid-afternoon the following day, I was entering the state of Georgia.

DREAMLAND MELODY

1

The devil appeared to me for the first time when I was ten. My father had left my mother and me at a friend's house where my mother was meeting a group of housewives to play *canasta*. Since there were no other children, I entertained myself roaming around the palatial chalet, bored to death, afraid to touch anything; it all looked so proper, so delicate, so expensive. But then it happened as I entered a dark, large room. Right in front of me, almost glowing, I saw this perfect woman, white and soft as meringue, she had a dreamy look about her, but what caught my eyes was something I had never seen before: a perfect pair of breasts. I approached her and examined every inch of her perfect body. I touched one of her nipples with the tip of my fingers, it was cold as ice, but she didn't move; I placed my whole hand over one of the breasts, and then—this is how I know it was the devil's fault—I put the breast in my mouth; it was hard like a rock, but it had a perfect form, and it felt great between my lips.

2

A few weeks after that, my father had left us. He went to the North; I didn't know where that was, but I was told he would send for us soon. Meanwhile, my mother and I were to stay with my father's parents. I couldn't understand that, since my father's parents were like strangers to me. I had actually spent most of my life in the house of my mother's parents. I remember one day when I was awakened by my grandmother's cries. I sat up on the bed; the room was dark but through the half-opened door I saw my grandfather running toward the patio holding a large kitchen knife in his hand. The backyard, together with three adjoining

ones, formed a huge orchard with oranges, mangos and a variety
of fruit trees. From the commotion, I realized that everyone in
the house had joined whatever was going on. The shouts of the
family had brought out all of the neighbors, who were not about
to miss a scandal no matter what time of night it happened to be.
Barefoot, and wearing only my white cotton underwear, I followed
the crowd. "Miguelito, go back, go back, stay in bed." It was the
voice of my mother, but I couldn't see where it was coming from.
The bright moon created monsters against the sky out of the fruit
trees.

"Armando, let him go, Armando," my grandmother, who was a
short, skinny woman in her late fifties, was shouting at my grandfather. The ground was cold and humid. I couldn't really see what
was going on, so I climbed a mango tree—which was a daily, after
school routine for me—in an attempt to look over the heads of the
neighbors. The women of the house—my grandmother, my mother
and her younger sister—were all exhorting my grandfather to stop
it. But I couldn't see what they wanted him to stop. My father, as
usual, was not home yet, and my uncle Miguel, after whom I was
named, was in the countryside that week. "Dad, let him go, please
let him go," my aunt was pleading, but my grandfather was in no
mood to listen to reason. He had cornered his son-in-law who had
his back to a wire fence.

"Son-of-a-bitch, I'll kill you!" he cried while gesturing with the
knife. "No one hits a daughter of mine."

My mother and her younger sister rushed to the old man, and,
as my aunt Nena pleaded with her father, my mother wrestled
the knife from his hand. My grandmother joined the family trio in
their desperate embrace, and all four fell to the ground among cries
and tears. "You better leave and don't come back!" my grandfather continued, cursing his son-in-law. "If I see you again around
my daughter I'll kill you, you hear me? I'll kill you!" The son-in-
law, who seemed to be quite drunk, as he was most of the time,
staggered out of the family's midnight circus and disappeared. The
neighbors, who up to that time had been satisfied to remain as spec-
tators, helped the group to their feet. My grandfather, still cursing
in his Galician dialect made his way back to the house; my grandmother followed, trying to gather the chickens awakened by the
family quarrel. Finally, the three sisters, embracing and consoling
each other, assured the neighbors that all was fine, that they could
go back to sleep, that thank you very much, that we'll see you tomorrow, that he was drunk, that please forgive the disturbance. My
aunt's dress was torn to pieces; she was bleeding from the mouth,

and one eye was swollen and half-closed. Fireflies made undulating designs in their flight, and a symphony of grasshoppers accompanied the family as it retreated. This was only the prelude to the purgatory they would endure, each in their own stoic manner, in their respective conjugal odysseys.

No matter how close I was to my mother's family, as long as my father was in the North, we were to remain at his parent's home. I was only ten years old, but to me they were not only strangers, but strange as well.

MEMORIES OF MY FATHER'S FAMILY

DURING HIS SELF-IMPOSED EXILE

ACT I

.... Scene 1 ....

A dining area and living room in a middle-class home. MARIO *is sitting by the radio, listening to a waltz by Strauss.* ANA *is doing housework in the kitchen.* ELENA *enters.*

ELENA: You're here already? It must be lunchtime.

ANA: (*From the kitchen*) You're having breakfast? (ELENA *picks up articles of clothing from the furniture*) It's almost noon. Everyone eats whenever they want. What do they care.

ELENA: A mother who talks to herself, a brother who doesn't talk. The three of us can make great conversation together.

ANA: (*Talking to herself*) I'm tired of making breakfast, of asking people if they want breakfast. (*Shouting at* ELENA) I asked you if you want breakfast?

ELENA: Of course I want breakfast.

MARIO: (*Talking to himself aloud*) Have you ever noticed how your hair sticks up in the back when you get up in the morning? If I don't wet my hair in the morning, I can't comb it. It goes to one side, like this, as if my head were a crooked pyramid.

ELENA: (*Sitting at the table*) It is.

MARIO: But I only wash it twice a week; the other days I just wet it.

ANA: (*Coming into the room*) I don't know what to make for lunch. Beto always wants chicken with rice. It's enough to have it on Sundays. I'll make *picadillo*. (*To* ELENA) You want *picadillo* for lunch?

ELENA: You know very well I never eat *picadillo*. In thirty-five years I have never had *picadillo*. Why do you ask me if I want *picadillo*?

MARIO: We heard you. You don't want *picadillo*.

ANA: Well, I'll make *picadillo*.

ELENA: I have such a headache. Why doesn't Otilio come with my prescription? I don't know why they trust a drunk with medicine.

ANA: He's not a drunk. He drinks a little, but that doesn't mean he is a drunk. Dr. Pérez gave him a place to live, and Otilio runs errands for him.

ELENA: (*Having breakfast*) Where's Lundi?

ANA: At five this morning he ran out of the house.

ELENA: If he continues like this, we'll have to put him in an institution.

ANA: We're not going to put him anywhere; what's gotten into you?

ELENA: Nothing has gotten into me. I'm just sick and tired of being the only one who works in this house. Do you know how many dresses and blouses I have to sell in that dump to keep this house going?

ANA: Roberto also gives money.

ELENA: Oh, yes! Roberto also gives money. When he wins at poker or blackjack. How about when he loses? Should we sit with a rosary, and pray for him to win? We're going to need lots of praying. This last year he's had a hell of a losing streak.

MARIO: That's strange! Roberto is a good gambler, he used to win all the time.

ANA: Leave him alone. You're always picking on your brothers. Stop it!

MARIO: A man was killed last night.

ELENA: I should put a stop to it. We'll all starve. How long has it been since Beto stopped working? What am I saying? He has never worked.

MARIO: In the middle of the night.

ANA: He worked when we had the farm.

ELENA: What are you talking about? He was the only farmer I
      know who never got dirt on his hands.

MARIO: I think they said it was something he ate.

ELENA: You know very well he sold the farm so that he wouldn't
      have to look for any more excuses not to work.

MARIO: What was it? I think it was *picadillo.* Pancho told me
      this morning. Do you know he lost his job? Pancho, I
      mean.

ELENA: I can't stand it when you do that.

MARIO: Do what?

ELENA: Start to say something, and then go into something else.

MARIO: I never do that.

ELENA: You just did it.

MARIO: The thing is that his wife said she made *picadillo* for
      dinner, that it was quite good, that she is a great cook and
      so on and so forth. But she also said that her husband was
      complaining it was too salty. And there's nothing worse
      than a salty *picadillo.* Well, to make a long story short ...

ELENA: Thank God for small favors. You never speak, but when
      you do ...

MARIO: To make a long story short ...

ELENA: I wonder where Lundi is.

MARIO: He ate the *picadillo.* In the middle of the night, the salty
      picadillo began to take revenge on him. He had to get up
      to go to the kitchen and get a glass of water. The usual
      nightly shooting that we've been having lately took place
      precisely at that moment. How lucky can you get? A
      bullet went through the kitchen window, and poor Chucho
      got it between the salty *picadillo* and the glass of water.

ANA: Is that the Chucho that's married to Felicia?

ELENA: Ana, the one that was married to Felicia, died two years
      ago.

ANA: How can that be?

ELENA: He was run over by a truck.

MARIO: Ana, watch the salt!

ELENA: If it's on account of the salt, no one will ever get shot in
      this house. She never uses salt.

ANA: Who says I don't use salt? Of course I use salt. How can I
      cook without salt. The thing is that in this house no one
      is ever satisfied.

ELENA: Salt or no salt your cooking leaves a lot to be desired. (
      LUNDI *enters running*)

LUNDI: It exploded. There was an explosion. Boom! An explosion. Didn't you hear it?

ELENA: What explosion?

ANA: I did hear something this morning.

LUNDI: An explosion, boom. I was there.

MARIO: I heard it on the news a little while ago.

LUNDI: People were running.

MARIO: Did anyone get killed?

ELENA: One day we'll all be blown to pieces. (*Leaving*) My head is splitting.

LUNDI: Mario, did you hear about the explosion?

MARIO: Yes, I heard about it on the radio. Did you hear about the shootings? They shot Chucho in the middle of the night.

LUNDI: In the middle of the night? I'm not sleeping anymore. No sir, not me. I'm not crazy. I'm going to be awake all night. All night. With my eyes open. Can you sleep with your eyes open? I better not, just in case. I have a better idea: I won't sleep anymore. Can I do that, Mario? Ana, Ana, can't I stop sleeping? Come on, Ana, help me to stop sleeping.

ANA: You can stop sleeping.

LUNDI: I'll just sit up all night. Mario, are you going to stop sleeping also? Eh, Mario, are you going to sit up all night?

ANA: Lundi, you have to go to the butcher.

LUNDI: To the butcher? You want meat?

ANA: No, I want potatoes.

LUNDI: The butcher doesn't sell potatoes, Ana. You're going crazy.

ANA: You're driving me crazy. You're driving everyone around here crazy. Now, listen. Stay put, and listen. Get a pound-and-a-half of ground beef for the *picadillo*.

LUNDI: Ground beef. A pound-and-a-half.

ANA: A pound-and-a-half.

LUNDI: Ground beef.

ANA: Yes.

LUNDI: A pound-and-a-half.

ANA: Of ground beef.

LUNDI: Ana, you sound like a broken record. Yes, a pound-and
   . . .

ANA: Hurry up, it's for lunch. (LUNDI *leaves, running.* BETO *enters. He's slender, pale. He's always whistling or making some sort of sound with his mouth. He wears a hat too small for his head.*)

BETO: One day that boy is going to stomp over someone. Where's he going?

ANA: To the butcher.

BETO: At this hour?

ANA: There was no one else.

BETO: Are we having chicken with rice?

ANA: We're having *picadillo.*

MARIO: (*Getting up*) Watch the salt.

BETO: What's with the salt?

ANA: Don't pay any attention to him.

BETO: Listening to so much music is making him stupid. (OTILIO *enters. He's unshaven. He's wearing very old clothes, but clean. He's drunk*)

OTILIO: Good people of Oriente. Permit me to call you Orientals, although if that were the case ...

ANA: Good morning, Otilio.

BETO: How did you come in?

OTILIO: My good man, permit me to call you inquisitive. Through the door, of course. (ELENA *enters*)

ELENA: You certainly took your time getting here. Did you bring my pills?

OTILIO: You may change that question into an affirmative statement.

ELENA: Thank God.

OTILIO: Do you believe that a Christian in harmony with God would need to consume such a fertile amount of manmade relief?

ELENA: What have you been drinking?

OTILIO: The nectar of forgiveness.

ELENA: Is that what they call it now?

OTILIO: Permit me to call you a pill freak.

ELENA: Otilio, I'm not in the mood.

OTILIO: My dear woman, that is the story of every mortal soul. One is never in the mood for what one gets. But one gets it anyway. Your days have been carved in the tree of life.

ELENA: Who do you think you are, the Aristotle of the Caribbean?

BETO: Otilio, for a Saturday morning you are really a pain in the neck.

OTILIO: Saturday mornings are no different than Wednesday afternoons, or Tuesday evenings.

ANA: You can say that again.

OTILIO: You are born into a circle.

ANA: You want some coffee?

OTILIO: That is poison. Although, if you have a bit of spirits.

BETO: There's no liquor in the house.

ANA: No one drinks here.

OTILIO: Allow me to call you cheap and dry.

ELENA: You have no place to go?

OTILIO: We are all confined to the place we inhabit. There's no escape, we're trapped.

ELENA: The door is open.

OTILIO: (*Takes a bottle from his coat pocket, pours into the cap and drinks*) Permit me to fertilize my soul. As I was saying, doors are deceiving.

OTILIO: Sometimes even open doors cannot let you escape, sometimes open doors trap you.

ELENA: Otilio, I have a headache.

OTILIO: That is just what I mean.

ELENA: Nothing that silence won't cure.

OTILIO: Words are incommunicable anyhow. Just sit back and relax.

ELENA: I wasn't talking about my silence. I was talking about yours.

ANA: Nena, don't be rude.

OTILIO: It's quite all right. We must all speak our peace sometime. I was leaving anyway. (*He starts to walk out*) I shall remember your faces as I see them now. (*To* ELENA) Permit me to call you a winter frog. Winter frogs are always lonely and make horrible sounds. (OTILIO *leaves*)

ELENA: I can't stand that man.

BETO: You can't stand anybody.

ELENA: I simply cannot stand drunks.

BETO: You simply hate people.

ANA: Nena always gets annoyed at the slightest thing.

BETO: I have never come across a man you happen to like.

ELENA: Certainly not in this house.

ANA: She was quite taken by that man, what was his name? Carlitos? Julito? You know, the nephew of Modesto, the barber.

ELENA: Let's not bring that up again.

BETO: That's who she likes: nobodies.

ELENA: Sure, that's the type I like, but you don't like any type. No one is good enough for you. Every time I met someone,

you rejected him. You always found some fault. (LUNDI
   enters)

ANA: Nena, the truth is you never met anyone who was worth
   anything.

ELENA: What am I supposed to be? A Cuban princess?

BETO: You may not be a princess, but you come from a good
   family.

ELENA: That's a laugh. All I know is that I am thirty-five and
   counting.

LUNDI: And counting fast. Thirty-five, thirty-six, thirty-seven.
   Am I good enough for you, Nena? Am I?

ELENA: Sure you are, Lundi.

BETO: If you haven't married it's your own fault.

ELENA: Let's drop it.

BETO: It's true.

ELENA: I don't know why you were always so particular about my
   going out with anyone. You are a disgrace yourself.

ANA: Elena.

LUNDI: Elena.

BETO: There's no more respect in this house.

ANA: You have no right to speak to him like that.

ELENA: It's the truth. What does he have to be so proud of?
   The only thing he has ever done is gamble at that club.
   He hasn't done an honest day's work in his life. And
   Roberto? A chip off the same block, a gambler like his
   father. Who's kidding whom?

BETO: You always had everything.

ELENA: Hell is what I've always had.

LUNDI: (*Singing*) Hell, hell, hell. Hell for everyone.

ANA: I better make lunch. Roberto is coming in a little while.

ELENA: Why don't you ask him to get married and work like any
   decent man should do. Oh, no! Not King Roberto. King
   Roberto is our beloved forty-year-old money-getter; the
   quickest hands in the tropics, the wizard of dominoes,
   our poker perfectionist.

ANA: Leave Roberto alone. He hasn't done anything to you.

ELENA: No, he hasn't done anything to me. He simply hasn't
   done anything. Why do you protect him all the time?
   Why do you always take sides with him?

ANA: I never take sides.

ELENA: You always do.

BETO: All right. All right. That's enough.

ELENA: It's not enough.

BETO: I said that's enough. (ELENA *rushes out*)

LUNDI: Beto, did you hear the explosion?

ANA: Lundi, cut it out.

BETO: What explosion?

LUNDI: There was an explosion, it went BOOM! You didn't hear it? You were probably asleep. Everybody else in town heard it, except you. But I swear, Beto, I had nothing to do with it.

ANA: Lundi, you have to get a haircut. Beto, give Lundi some money to get a haircut.

BETO: He looks fine to me.

LUNDI: I look fine,

ANA: If you don't get a haircut, you're not having lunch.

LUNDI: Beto, give me the money. Did I tell you about the explosion? Beto, I swear I had nothing to do with it.

BETO: I'm sure you didn't.

LUNDI: You believe me, Beto, don't you?

BETO: Why shouldn't I believe you?

LUNDI: I just wanted to make sure. (*Pause*) Do you know what I learned today? I learned that the rebels are in town.

BETO: Where did you hear that?

LUNDI: You know who is a rebel? Martinez, the man who works at the bank.

ANA: (*Entering*) Where did you hear that?

LUNDI: I heard it, I heard it. There's going to be such an explosion. I heard everything.

ANA: My head is what's going to explode.

LUNDI: Ana, you know they say that the jails are full. Full, full, full, full. And you know what? They pull out their fingernails to make them talk.

ANA: Where have you been that you heard all this?

LUNDI: I know.

BETO: If some rebels get caught, I'm sure they'll do anything to make them say whatever they want to hear. That's war.

ANA: What war?

BETO: Ana, people are getting killed all over. Look what happened to that guy Chucho. He got killed in his own home, drinking a glass of water.

ANA: That's no war, it's just a bunch of crazy soldiers.

LUNDI: I'll talk. If they ask me, I'll talk.

ANA: You have nothing to say, you know nothing.

LUNDI: Yes I do. I heard the explosion. I saw everything.

ANA: You were imagining things.

LUNDI: I wasn't imagining things. Beto, do you believe I was imagining things? You said you believed me, didn't you?

BETO: Yes, I believe you, Lundi, but you can't go around telling people you know anything.

LUNDI: But, if they send me to jail?

ANA: Nobody is going to send you any place, except to take out the garbage.

LUNDI: But if they send me to jail, I'll talk. No, you're right, I don't know anything. I won't talk. Right, Beto?

ANA: I want to know where you've been.

LUNDI: Here and there.

ANA: You should spend more time here, instead of running around the city looking for bombs.

BETO: Lundi, you have nothing to worry about, the white horse hasn't been seen yet.

ANA: You fantasize more than he does.

LUNDI: What white horse, Beto?

BETO: You don't know the legend of the white horse?

LUNDI: No, but I want to know. Tell me about it, Beto. Tell me, tell me.

BETO: Well, the story goes like this: When the Spanish first started to settle in Cuba, they sent a man called Don Alfonso de Ojeda to our town. Well, this guy Don Alfonso had a very beautiful daughter. Then there was this Indian, a very handsome man. He used to ride a white horse every afternoon. The Spanish made the Indians work all day, but since Cueiba was a very strong Indian, he would always finish early, and then he would go around town on his beautiful white horse. One day he saw the daughter of Ojeda, and he fell in love with her, and she also fell in love with him. But it was an impossible love. So one night he ran away with her, and he was caught.

LUNDI: Did they pull out his fingernails?

BETO: Forget about the fingernails. He was beheaded. They cut off his head.

LUNDI: I don't want them to cut off my head.

BETO: Will you listen? Well, after that, the beheaded Indian rode around town on his white horse. Now, every time that something happens, some tragedy or something, they say they see the white horse prancing along Francisco Vega Street.

LUNDI: I don't know, Beto, but I don't have a white horse. I don't want them to cut off my head. Beto, don't let them cut off my head.

ANA: Now you've really fixed things.

LUNDI: I would look horrible without my head. (LUNDI *starts to leave*) I want my head. I want my head. I want ...
(LUNDI *runs out shouting*)

ANA: Lundi, come back here.

BETO: Let him go.

ANA: How can I let him go? He's going to get into trouble. Lundi! Beto, go after him. Lundi! Beto, go and get him back.

BETO: I have to work on my list, it's been a slow day.

ANA: I don't care, go after him. Beto, he has to go to the butcher. Go after him or there will be no lunch.

BETO: (*Getting up*) When it isn't lunch, dinner; it's always something. (*He walks out*)

ANA: I would be very happy if I didn't have to cook. We can forget about it right now. Less work for me. Forty years cooking three meals a day. How many meals is that? If I only knew. I wonder why women want to get married; you're either a housewife, an old maid or a prostitute. I don't know which is worse. (*Pause*) Don't go to the store. Don't do anything. Leave it to me. I do the cooking, the cleaning, the laundry. (ELENA *enters*)

ELENA: You're talking to yourself again.

ANA: I'm talking to your father.

ELENA: Where is he?

ANA: He's around.

ELENA: There's no one here.

ANA: That's the way he solves everything, by leaving. He has spent his whole life walking away from everything.

ELENA: You're in good form today.

ANA: The best thing you can do is never to marry anyone.

ELENA: The prospects are not very good, so you don't have to worry.

ANA: You're better off.

ELENA: Sure, I'm better off. I spend my days working in a rathole of a store, and my evenings sitting on that porch watching people go by, watching my life go by. I'm a professional spectator. Everything passes me by.

ANA: It could be worse.

ELENA: Certainly it could be worse. You tell me how it could be worse. I am thirty-five years old. Thirty-five years old and I have never felt a caress. Not once has a man touched my hair.

ANA: Why do you want anybody to touch your hair?

ELENA: I don't know what it is to have someone hold my hand. To have someone talk to me.

ANA: Here everybody talks to you.

ELENA: Here everybody talks to himself. Besides, what everyone says around here is not worth hearing.

ANA: Believe me, you've missed nothing. I remember the first time your father held my hand. He didn't say a word. Well, he has never said much, that's nothing new. We were walking in the park on a Sunday afternoon. The municipal band was playing. You know that the men walk in one direction and the women in the opposite direction. Well, we had gone around the park six or seven times. Everytime we passed each other he would smile. He was wearing his little hat, just like the one he wears now. About the eighth time he said something, I don't know what. He just mumbled something. The next time around we stopped as we were about to pass each other by. He mumbled something again, and grabbed one of my fingers. I nearly died. I was petrified. Everybody was looking at us. I pulled my hand back and walked away as fast as my legs could carry me. I was almost running. My face was red as a tomato. But after that, it was all downhill.

ELENA: I would have been happy with just that moment. (*Fade-out*)

.... Scene 2 ....

That evening, ELENA, ANA, BETO *and* ROBINSON *are seated on the porch, watching people go by.*

ROBINSON: People are all the same. You've seen how the situation has deteriorated in the last two years; nobody seems to mind. They go about their business, as if nothing is happening. Everyone works, plays, drinks. Nothing bothers the people here.

BETO: Talking about playing, Nico owes me $2.50. He played a pretty combination.

ROBINSON: What was it?

BETO: He dreamed he was taking a long voyage by sea, but there was no ship. All there was was a horse. So, what did he do? He bets on #1 and #3; horse and sailor, a great combination.

ANA: That's really far-fetched.

ROBINSON: It's a common dream.

ANA: Going to sea on a horse?

ROBINSON: Everyone has a story.

BETO: There was nothing wrong with the combination, although it didn't win.

ROBINSON: Take me, for instance.

ELENA: Who would want to take you, Robinson?

ROBINSON: One day I'm reading the newspaper, and what do I find? Right there, on page seven I read that I'm dead. Dead. No more, no less.

BETO: You should play number sixty-four: "Big-dead-man," and number four for cat, with nine lives. That's a pretty combination: four and sixty-four.

ROBINSON: I mean, how would you feel reading that you're dead?

ELENA: We're all dead, we've all been dead forever. Everyone in this town. Life never came here.

ANA: Nena, you say such things.

BETO: Maybe you should play eight, instead of sixty four.

ELENA: Stop it with your numbers. All you think about is numbers, combinations, gambling, cockfights.

BETO: Just because you play every day and never win is no reason to criticize the ones who do.

ELENA: Some people are not lucky at gambling, but they're lucky at love, or vice-versa. I lost on both counts.

ROBINSON: As I was saying, I was reading this newspaper, and there I found my name: Raul Robinson, dead.

ANA: You don't look dead to me, Robinson.

ROBINSON: Thank God.

ELENA: Someone probably took a look at you, and decided you had one foot on the other side.

ROBINSON: No, really, I'm not kidding.

ANA: But how can that be?

ROBINSON: Well, I left Havana quite some time ago, and I never went back.

ANA: That's no reason to kill you.

ROBINSON: No, but I never wrote back. I never got in touch with anyone.

BETO: Well, that was very foolish.

ELENA: Come to think of it, why did you come here in the first place? Of all the places to go, you came here.

ROBINSON: I wanted to get away from everything.

ELENA: You came to the right place.

ANA: What made you want to get away?

ROBINSON: My wife died. I ... I sort of went crazy. I didn't
have anyone else. We didn't have any children. We were
always together, for thirty years.

BETO: I didn't have such luck.

ANA: I don't know what you would have done without me.

ELENA: The same thing he has done with you. Nothing.

BETO: But you were very well-known, weren't you, Robinson?

ROBINSON: Yeah, I made a name for myself. I was a composer.

ANA: Of music?

BETO: Sure. You had some pieces that were famous.

ROBINSON: Well, from this incident that I told you about, I wrote
a *danzón* that became very popular: "Alive and Kicking,"
that was the title.

BETO: I have danced to that many times.

ANA: Not with me.

BETO: That was before your time.

ANA: I've never danced in my life.

ELENA: That's one thing we have in common.

ROBINSON: That's a shame. My wife and I used to go dancing
every week.

ANA: Maybe you two can go out dancing sometime?

ELENA: You must be crazy.

ROBINSON: That's not a bad idea. I can still get around the dance
floor.

BETO: I wonder what number is dancing.

ANA: I don't think dancing has a number.

ROBINSON: Dancing? Three-quarter.

ANA: Three-quarter?

ROBINSON: Sure. Three-quarter, like a waltz. La, la-la, la, la-la.

ELENA: Speaking of waltzes, your music-loving son didn't come
to dinner tonight.

ANA: He wasn't feeling well.

ELENA: Could it have been from indigestion?

ANA: He has a great stomach.

ELENA: That, I'll agree with you.

ROBINSON: That's Mario you're talking about? He knows his
music all right.

ELENA: That's the only thing he knows.

ANA: He knows a lot about electricity.

ROBINSON: It's hard to make a living in this town.

ELENA: If you want to work, you can find it.

ROBINSON: Not me, I'm okay. I have a few pennies in the bank.

ANA: Nena should have married a responsible man like you, Robinson. (ROBINSON *chuckles*, ELENA *gives a piercing glance at her mother*)

BETO: The house has been quiet without Lundi.

ROBINSON: He hasn't shown up yet?

ANA: He vanished. No one has seen him, no one knows anything.

BETO: It was going to happen sooner or later. A crazy boy running around town day and night with the way things are. Maybe he went to the mountains to join the rebels.

ANA: What does he know about the rebels?

BETO: The same thing that we do: nothing. Nena, don't you think it's possible?

ELENA: I don't want to talk about it. If anything happens to him, it's our fault.

ANA: Why is it our fault?

ELENA: We drove him crazy.

ANA: What's this guilt feeling that's come over you?

ELENA: You disgust me.

ANA: Stop it, we have visitors.

ELENA: Robinson knows what goes on in this house. Besides, I have been stopping all my life. I'm tired of living with lies.

ANA: You live the life you want to live.

ELENA: I have lived the life you made me live.

ANA: What would you have done without me.

ELENA: Been a normal human being. You made freaks of us all.

ANA: Blame me for everything. I'm sure you're going to blame me for Lundi's madness also?

ELENA: Yes, I'll blame you for everything. We were all your scapegoats. Don't play victim with me. You've been doing that for too long.

BETO: You have no reason to say that.

ELENA: Don't you preach to me. It's too late for that. You're too old to begin to act like a man now. (*Pause*)

ANA: Robinson, don't get the wrong impression, we all loved Lundi. He grew up in our house. When he was little, his parents moved to Havana. They were living in a small apartment, so they asked us to attend to him for a few weeks, until they got settled. Since he was the brother-in-law of Hilda, my daughter, we said yes. So he came to live with us. It was supposed to be temporary. His parents left for the United States, and he's been here ever since. Ah, Robinson ... (*Shots are heard at a distance*)

ROBINSON: There goes the shootings again. Do you know that Polanco put some hooks on the bathroom walls to hang mattresses when the shootings start? They're living half their lives in the bathroom. We're all nervous. Myself? I stare at the walls at night. I can't sleep.

ELENA: Lundi used to stare at the walls.

ANA: Let's stop talking about Lundi. (*Leaving*) Good night.

ELENA: Yes, let's stop talking about Lundi. Let's simply stop talking.

ANA: You're becoming impossible. (*Pause*)

ROBINSON: Well, I must be going. It's getting late, and you know it's not safe to walk the streets at night.

BETO: Yeah, I think I'm going to turn in also.

ROBINSON: (*Leaving*) Good night.

BETO: (*Leaving in the opposite direction*) Good night, Robinson. Remember, tomorrow is Saturday. Try to dream of a winner.

ANA: Good night. (*To* ELENA) You should be ashamed of yourself.

ELENA: For saying the truth? It's strange to hear the truth around here. It's about time we started, don't you think? Or I should say, it's about time you all started because I won't be here.

ANA: What do you mean?

ELENA: I mean I'm leaving.

ANA: Leaving for where?

ELENA: Leaving. Leaving for good. I'm going to the North.

ANA: You're crazy.

ELENA: Just like Lundi. (BETO *enters*)

BETO: Ana, my milk.

ANA: Beto, Elena's going to the North.

BETO: Yes, she needs to get away for a while.

ELENA: Not for a while, I have to do something with my life.

BETO: You have your job.

ELENA: Oh, yes, I should treasure selling old-fashioned dresses to old-fashioned women.

ANA: You have lots of friends.

ELENA: Three ugly women with whom I play *canasta*. I can always invite myself to some neighbor's house to watch television, or sit here and watch people go by.

BETO:. Well, you're old enough. You do what you think you have to do. I won't stop you.

ANA: What are people going to say? A woman traveling alone to the United States.

ELENA: You're in another century. This town, this country is in another century.

ELENA: There's a revolution going on out there. People are getting killed everyday. We have to sleep on the floor most of the time. They shoot at our houses. Everything's falling down, and you're still worried about my traveling alone, about what people are going to say. Damn the people, damn this town, this country, this revolution. Damn you, I'm leaving. (*She rushes out*)

ANA: I don't know what's come over this girl. (BETO *sits next to Ana*)

BETO: We wanted the best for her. We loved her. Didn't we?

ANA: She'll get over it in the morning.

BETO: She won't. She's been holding back for too many years. You know, Ana, I haven't mingled much in the affairs of this house, but I know what's been going on. I know she resents me. (*Pause*) I don't want to die knowing my daughter hates me. (*She holds his hand*)

ANA: Don't you start now. She's just tired. It will be all right. (BETO *gets up and walks out slowly. She stares into the distance and talks to herself*) Elena is right, this is a house of lunatics.

.... Scene 3 ....

Next morning. Dining room area. ELENA *and* MARIO *are having breakfast.* OTILIO *enters*

OTILIO: Good people of Oriente, permit me ...

ELENA: Otilio, you have great visiting hours.

OTILIO: As the Chinese philosopher once said ...

ELENA: Otilio, it's too early for philosophy.

OTILIO: Permit me to call you tired sun, for you are a slow riser.

ELENA: Permit me to show you to the door, for you are leaving.

MARIO: Jesus, I can't even have breakfast in peace.

ELENA: I'm kidding, Otilio.

OTILIO: I know, I know ... (*Pause*) Is it true that you're leaving?

ELENA: It's true.

MARIO: I don't think that's a good idea.

ELENA: You simply don't think.

MARIO: Listen to our precocious old maid.

ELENA: Why don't you just worry about your own family? Your wife is pregnant again, and still washing clothes to feed your children. How can you sit there like a tropical Buddha?

MARIO: And you are so pure! You are the one to be blamed for Lundi. Always complaining about him. Have you forgotten how you made fun of him, how you imitated him, how you used to put live frogs in his bed?

ELENA: Stop it.

MARIO: I thought you wanted to talk about Lundi?

ELENA: Stop it.

MARIO: Remember the time you were taking a shower, and you called Lundi to bring you a towel, and you let him see you naked, and then laughed at him?

ELENA: Stop it.

MARIO: You drove him crazy.

ELENA: Stop it, stop it.

MARIO: You want me to stop now?

ELENA: Mario. (ANA *and* BETO *enter carrying groceries*)

ANA: What's all this shouting? (*Pause*) We were just at the market. No one knows anything.

BETO: I want my steak medium rare.

ANA: We're not having steaks.

BETO: For forty years I've been telling her that I like my steaks medium-rare. I cannot eat a well-done steak. Elena, you know I cannot chew.

ANA: I wish Roberto were here.

BETO: (*Going to the bedroom*) Remember, medium-rare. (*A car is heard coming to a full stop. Doors slam. Voices are heard. The car skids off. LUNDI enters, with both hands bandaged, and full of blood stains*)

LUNDI: I didn't tell them.

ANA: Lundi, My God!

LUNDI: I didn't tell them, I didn't tell them, and they said I was lying. I didn't tell them, and they pulled out my fingernails. Ana, Beto, Nena, I didn't tell them, I didn't tell them. (LUNDI *collapses*)

ELENA: Lundi! (*Blackout*)

ACT II

.... Scene 1 ....

Miami, Florida, five years later. The living room of an small apartment. ROBERTO is sitting at a desk, writing. ELENA is sitting on the sofa, reading a magazine.

ELENA: Do you know what day it is today?
ROBERTO: Saturday.
ELENA: I mean, what day of the week?
ROBERTO: 17th.
ELENA: December 17th.
ROBERTO: So?
ELENA: Five years ago today Lundi died.
ROBERTO: It's been five years already?
ELENA: We arrived in Miami almost four years ago. It's funny
    how things worked out. I was going to leave Cuba in
    December of '58; then Lundi died; then Beto became ill;
    then the Revolution triumphed; then Beto also died, and
    then all of us left. Lundi was crazy, and yet he was the
    only one in our house who saw what was happening in
    Cuba.
ROBERTO: I knew what was happening. As it turned out, all
    the fighting was for nothing, that son-of-a-bitch turned
    communist on us. He really fooled everybody, didn't he?
ELENA: You kept your secret pretty well. No one ever suspected
    that you were a rebel. How could you keep something like
    that from us?
ROBERTO: I had to. I was doing sabotage, putting bombs all over
    Oriente. That was no child's play. They would have shot
    me on sight.
ELENA: How long did you do that?
ROBERTO: Since the middle of '57. Fidel was just sitting there
    in the mountains, nothing was happening, so we decided
    to take the fight to the towns. It was actually the sabotage
    in the cities that finally brought Batista's downfall.
ELENA: What do you mean?

ROBERTO: The soldiers began taking reprisals; in the process they
       hurt lots of innocent people. They began torturing people,
       some died. You never heard the cries in the night?

ELENA: No.

ROBERTO: They got very vicious.

ELENA: Pulling out people's fingernails?

ROBERTO: That was just the beginning.

ELENA: That's what happened to Lundi.

ROBERTO: It's always the innocents ...

ELENA: Did he know anything?

ROBERTO: About what?

ELENA: About anything: the rebels? You?

ROBERTO: What do you mean?

ELENA: You know what I mean. Did Lundi know that you were
      a rebel? Did he know that you were doing sabotage?

ROBERTO: What do I know? He was always showing up every-
       where.

ELENA: Did Lundi ever see you plant a bomb? Remember when
      he came to the house screaming about an explosion? Was
      that you? Did he see you?

ROBERTO: Maybe he saw me, I don't know.

ELENA: Maybe he saw you, and maybe he was caught, and maybe
      the soldiers interrogated him, and tortured him. Maybe
      they pulled out his fingernails when he didn't talk, because
      he knew it was you, and he wanted to protect you.

ROBERTO: (*Angry*) Yes, he saw me. What the hell was he doing
      there? He was not supposed to be there, it was six-o'clock
      in the morning ... (*Pause*) I took two sticks of dynamite
      and placed them at the door of the courthouse ... the
      whole place blew up; as I turned around the corner to get
      into the car that was waiting for me, there he was, looking
      at me with his big eyes, and a grin on his skinny face. I
      didn't say a word. I thought that in his craziness he would
      not realize what had happened ...

ELENA: But, why didn't you say something?

ROBERTO: I couldn't, Nena, believe me, I couldn't. After the
      triumph of the Revolution, I went to Mazorra to find out
      how he died. I met the man who was in charge of him. He
      just said that Lundi had gotten wild one night, while trying
      to control him, somebody must have hit him; he fell to the
      ground, hit his head against the cement wall and died ...
      I was sure that they had actually beaten him to death. He
      began making fun of the inmates, that they should all be

killed ... I saw that man as a savage, I thought he had to be destroyed, the Revolution could not afford people like that, so I took out my pistol and shot him. I was a captain in the Revolutionary Army. I was authorized to shoot anyone that I considered dangerous. When people came into the room to ask what had happened, I just said that he was a counter-revolutionary, and that I had executed him.

ELENA: You killed him just like that?

ROBERTO: Do you realize how many people were killed in '59 just like that? Anyone who had a grudge against someone else simply shot him. No questions asked. If a man found out that his wife was sleeping with another man, all he had to do was accuse his wife's lover of being a *gusano*, and then he would shoot him. We were in power, the law was on our side. We were *barbudos*, we came from the mountains, and we had a gun at our side. Thousands of people were killed.Want to know something? I never forgot Lundi's eyes looking at me; not questioning, nor judging, just looking at me. I close my eyes, and I see him, even now.

ELENA: Always someone has to die before we become aware of anything. I realized I loved Lundi when he died. And Beto, boy, I really mistreated him. I used to curse him, scream at him. I don't remember ever kissing him, my own father. Then he died, and I began to reproach myself ...

ROBERTO: Don't be so tough on yourself.

ELENA: Why shouldn't I. I was tough with everybody else. You were always away. We thought you were gambling, and you were putting bombs. I needed you so much.

ROBERTO: We're together now.

ELENA: I'm so tired ... (*Pause*) Ana is almost totally blind. I spoke with Dr. Porilla today. We'll have to watch her. Last night, after everyone had gone to bed I passed by her room, and she was lying in bed, crying.

ROBERTO: She must miss Beto. They got along; she knew how to handle him. They accepted each other, they understood each other. In their own way, they must have loved each other.

ELENA: I'm sure they did. Love is funny, don't you think? (*Fade-*

out)

·························· Scene 2 ··························

ANA *is standing by the window, looking out.* MARIO *enters.*
ANA: Where's Elena?
MARIO: I think she went to do the laundry. She can't stand still. Always complaining she's tired, but she doesn't stop working.
ANA: She doesn't stop because she doesn't want to have time to think. (MARIO *takes her by the arm, and walks her to the sofa*)
MARIO: About Ralph, you mean?
ANA: Since she was very young she always wanted to get married. She was always talking about marriage. Finally, she met Ralph, and she got her wish. She was so happy. I wish Beto had been alive. He felt guilty, he thought it had been his fault that Nena never married . He never showed it, but he loved all his children. He would have been so pleased to have seen Nena finally getting married. And Ralph was such a good man, so kind.
MARIO: It was the only time that I have seen her smile.
ANA: You never saw her smile because you always made her angry. You were always picking on her. She had a bad temper, she grew up too soon ... Besides, she could never accept the fact that you were married, and had children, and yet you came to have lunch and dinner with us.
MARIO: You always insisted.
ANA: I didn't want you to go hungry. Your wife was a horrible cook.
MARIO: I feel sorry for her.
ANA: You feel sorry for Nena? I don't see why.
MARIO: Remember when she brought him home for the first time? She was like a little girl, she was blushing. I thought she was going to die. She spilled her coffee, he didn't know what to say, you kept on asking questions ...
MARIO: It's a shame he died, but he always looked sick to me. Jesus, he had a green complexion.
ANA: He didn't have a green complexion.
MARIO: He didn't have pink cheeks either.
ANA: He had cancer. In Cuba I never heard of anyone having cancer. That's an American illness.

MARIO: They had cancer in Cuba. What happened is that in Cuba people died, and nobody knew from what.

ANA: People are too finicky here.

MARIO: You're too old-fashioned. Americans like things fast.

ANA: Yes, even death. (*A knock is heard at the door*)

MARIO: Come in. (OTILIO *enters wearing suit and tie, and quite sober*)

OTILIO: Good people of Oriente, good day!

MARIO: Otilio, Good Lord! You really put on the wardrobe.

ANA: Is that Otilio?

OTILIO: Alive and kicking, as that old song that made our friend Robinson so famous.

MARIO: How come you're so elegant?

OTILIO: Well, it's Saturday. So I said to myself, what the hell, I'll get myself elegant.

MARIO: Take a seat.

ANA: I don't know what got into you, because on Saturdays everyone around here dresses just the same as any other day.

OTILIO: To tell you the truth, I've decided to join the world of the conformists.

MARIO: You're getting married?

OTILIO: Oh, no, no, no. Nothing so drastic. I'm not conforming that much.

ANA: You should get married, Otilio, you're still young.

OTILIO: No thank you, Ana. Once is enough.

MARIO: If you're not getting married, what's the drastic change in your life?

OTILIO: I decided to go back to teaching.

ANA: You're a teacher?

OTILIO: I have always been one.

ANA: My God, the things one finds out in exile!

MARIO: That's why people used to call you professor in Tunas?

OTILIO: People called me professor to make fun of me. No, in Tunas only Dr. Pérez knew that I was a college professor before ...

MARIO: Before you started drinking?

OTILIO: Before I dropped out of our gracious tropical society, and began to indulge myself in liquor. Yes, before I started drinking.

ANA: I always wondered why you drank. You seemed perfectly healthy to me; young, even good-looking. My goodness, Otilio, you ruined your life.

OTILIO: It's a long story, Ana. I don't think you want to hear it.

ANA: Sure I want to hear it. I am going blind, but people must think that I am going deaf. Nobody wants to tell me anything.

MARIO: Ana, don't start that again.

ANA: Mario, I mean it. I am bored to death.

OTILIO: Don't worry, Ana. I'll talk to you. I'll tell you the story.

MARIO: (*To* OTILIO) Do you want some coffee?

OTILIO: Yes, thank you. Had someone ever told me that I was going to be in Miami drinking coffee, I would have told them that they were doubly crazy. I never touched the stuff in my life; and here I am, a coffee addict. (MARIO *returns with a cup of espresso coffee*)

MARIO: It's from this morning. I reheated it.

OTILIO: It's fine.

ANA: Otilio, I'm waiting. Tell me what happened?

OTILIO: I'm coming to that. (*He takes a sip from the coffee*) I am not from Las Tunas, as you must know.

ANA: I didn't know that.

OTILIO: No, I was born in Las Villas, in the central part of the island. I was a philosophy teacher. I was married.

ANA: Listen to that!

OTILIO: She was beautiful, much younger than I was. She was a girl from the countryside, full of life and zest, and we were happy. My students from the university used to come to the house, and we talked all through the night about John Locke, and Mañach, and Martí, and so on and so forth. But what I didn't know was that when I was teaching during the day, some of the students came back, and it wasn't to talk about philosophy. Of course, I was the last to know. When I finally found out, it was my own wife who told me.

ANA: She told you she was being unfaithful to you?

OTILIO: Not only that. She told me she was leaving me, and she did. She went to Havana with one of my students, José del Valle. He was writing his thesis at the time: "The Concept of Liberty in the New World".

MARIO: He certainly took his liberties!

OTILIO: He not only took his liberties, he took my wife.

ANA: And what did you do?

OTILIO: I went to pieces. I couldn't teach any longer, I couldn't do anything. I took to drinking; then I lost my job at the university. Finally, I decided to leave Las Villas. So I went to the other extreme of the island, and I wound up in Tunas.

MARIO: You can't trust women.

OTILIO: I don't know about that, Mario; but my Gladys really broke my heart. Can I tell you something? Do you know that I still love her? After all these years. And if I saw her today ... well ... I heard that she had left Cuba.

ANA: Do you want to see her?

OTILIO: I'd give anything to see her again. Just to see her. She had long, curly hair, and laughter. Oh, God! Ana why do you do this to me?

MARIO: My wife left me also.

OTILIO: What? I thought you left her?

MARIO: No, she left me. I shouldn't have married anyhow. I wasn't made to have a family.

OTILIO: It certainly took you a long time to figure that one out. You had four or five children, no?

MARIO: I have five. They're all still in Cuba, in the army. They're all communists.

OTILIO: I'm sure they're better off.

ANA: That's a terrible thing to say, Otilio, but you haven't told us why you're so elegant.

OTILIO: I'm going back to teaching. I got an offer to teach Spanish, grammar and so on. So, I'm celebrating my return to the classroom. I stopped drinking. Well, I drink less. I'll leave you now.

ANA: Don't go. Elena will be back in a minute; she'll be very happy to see you.

OTILIO: I'd like to see her also, Ana, but I don't think that I am ready. Give me time.

ANA: As you wish; this is your home. Do come more often. It would be nice having someone to talk to again. I remember when you used to come to our house in Tunas and talk for hours.

OTILIO: I will come more often, Ana. I promise.

MARIO: Next time I'll make you fresh coffee. (*Blackout*)

.... Scene 3 ....

MARIO *is sitting by the radio.* ANA *is standing by the door, looking out.* ELENA, *wearing rubber gloves, is cleaning. The television set is on. From the radio a waltz is heard.*

ELENA: (*To* MARIO) Sooner or later you will have to get up from
　　　there. I have to clean that corner.

MARIO: What for?

ELENA: What a question.

MARIO: Nobody is going to come looking under my seat.

ELENA: God help the one who does.

MARIO: So, you don't have to clean here.

ELENA: Mario, don't get me started.

MARIO: Why don't you go home?

ELENA: Yes, I should go home, and you will die in filth. If it
　　　weren't for Ana ...

ANA: I'll clean that later.

ELENA: You'll clean that later. You cannot accept the fact that
　　　you're almost blind. How can you clean anything? Mario,
　　　get up.

MARIO: Will you please be quiet? I'm listening to music.

ANA: Nena, I'll clean that.

ELENA: You're so hard-headed!

ANA: Look who's calling whom hard-headed.

ELENA: (*To* MARIO) If you're not watching the TV, why do you
　　　have it on?

MARIO: I'm watching it.

ELENA: Without sound?

MARIO: I said I'm watching it, not listening to it.

ELENA: (*Taking her mother by the arm*) Come and sit for a while.

ANA: I have to make lunch for Roberto.

ELENA: Today's Saturday, he's at his numbers game.

MARIO: But he always comes home for lunch.

ELENA: For once he should make his own.

ANA: I have some meat in the refrigerator, from last night.

ELENA: I'll do it.

ANA: How Beto would have loved to have had meat on Saturday!

ELENA: He had his share.

ANA: We couldn't afford to buy meat more than once a week when
　　　he was alive.

ELENA: He had an easy enough life.

ANA: Sometimes an easy life is not easy.

ELENA: I'll take it any day!

ANA: Don't worry, we won't be here much longer.

ELENA: Stop dreaming, we're here for good.

ANA: Not me. I know I won't die here. And if I do, I already made
　　　your brother promise that I would be buried in Cuba.

ELENA: Once you're dead, what difference does it make?

ANA: It makes a lot of difference. I don't belong here. We don't belong here.

ELENA: We don't belong anywhere, we have lost our place in the world.

MARIO: Maybe you have, because you have no faith. It's because of people like you that we are in exile.

ELENA: We got what we deserved.

ANA: I cannot believe that we deserved this. We lost our home, our friends, our family.

ELENA: That's a small price to pay. Even now, we haven't learned our lesson.

ANA: Anyway, I am certain that by next Christmas we'll be in Cuba.

ELENA: For five years we've been saying that: Next Christmas we'll be in Cuba. Christmases come and go, but we're still here.

MARIO: We'll never be Americans.

ELENA: We'll never be anything.

ANA: I live in the past, Nena, because it's all I have, it helps me to live the present. But with you it's different, you still have a future.

ELENA: Ana, I was born out of place, out of time. Even if I wanted to, even if I tried, I couldn't get anywhere.

ANA: Of course you can. I wish I was your age.

ELENA: We always wish what we cannot be. We always want what we cannot have. Maybe it's a defense mechanism. If we wish something very remote, we'll never be disillusioned, we'll never chastise ourselves for being a failure.

ANA: You're not a failure, you're a woman. If you just stopped feeling sorry for yourself for a moment, you would see that. Fight for what you want. I haven't given you much. At least take my strength.

ELENA: That's enough. God must be punishing me. In Cuba I used to complain because you didn't talk, now you talk too much.

ANA: It's all I can do.

MARIO: You don't look well.

ELENA: You're nothing to write home about.

MARIO: You're not so old.

ELENA: Coming from you, that's quite a compliment. I really have a monopoly on tragedy, don't I? Married at 38, widowed at 40.

ANA: Ralph was ill, you have nothing to blame yourself for.

MARIO: At least you were married for two years.

ELENA: Two wonderful years. The only time in my life I was really happy. He was so good to me! He made me feel needed. It's a great feeling to be needed.

ANA: I told you that you should marry again.

ELENA: I can't do that.

MARIO: Why not? You are your own worst enemy, always defeating yourself. Stop feeling sorry for yourself.

ELENA: And you stop talking, and get up. (*Pause*)

ANA: Miami is really much hotter than Tunas.

MARIO: (*Getting up*) I'm going to the bathroom.

ELENA: Ana, what a short memory you have. That little house we had on Lucas Ortiz Avenue was hell, a Cuban oven.

ANA: It wasn't so bad. At night there was always a breeze.

ELENA Yes, a warm breeze. Remember when I was going to leave home and go to New York?

ANA: That was a crazy idea.

ELENA: I never got to see New York.

ANA: We came to Miami because it was the closest thing to Cuba.

ELENA: That, it is. I've come a long way: from a clothing store to a restaurant at a racetrack. A real success story.

ANA: Sit down for a while, your back is going to start hurting you again.

ELENA: I have to finish cleaning. I still have to go home and clean there, also.

ANA: You live alone because you want to. It was all right for you to move out when you got married, we had no room here for both of you. But now you could very well move back here, unless you plan to get married again.

ELENA: It's not likely. It took me almost forty years to marry the first time. If I have to wait another forty years, I don't think I'll be in the mood for it.

ANA: You're better off. Men are a nuisance.

ELENA: You ought to know. You took care of three for years. It's about time Roberto got married. He's fifty, no?

ANA: Beto? Let me see. Yes, he's the oldest.

ELENA: It's about time he left home also.

ANA: He won't know how to take care of himself.

ELENA: Beautiful.

ANA: It's not his fault; he always had someone to do things for him.

ELENA: Yes, he had you, and Amparo. Poor Amparo. For twenty years they saw each other. She cooked for him every

Thursday for twenty years; she made handkerchiefs for
him. Can you imagine? After twenty years of putting up
with him, he leaves the country and she stays behind.

ANA: She wasn't in love with him.

ELENA: How can you say that? She was with him for twenty
years, without being married to him even, and you think
that she wasn't in love with him?

ANA: They were probably used to each other. People get used to
each other after a while.

ELENA: She was certainly used. (MARIO *comes in*)

MARIO: Are you finished?

ELENA: Yes.

ANA: There's no milk.

MARIO: No milk?

ANA: You had what was left this morning.

MARIO: Ana, you should make sure we never run out.

ELENA: Why don't you make sure.

MARIO: Why don't you mind your own business. (MARIO *leaves*)

ANA: That boy doesn't change.

ELENA: There were always two things we could count on:
Roberto's gambling and Mario's music. His wife left him,
his sons grew up, two or three governments fell, we left
the country, our father died, and all through it he was
listening to music, to his dreamland melody.

ANA: (*Getting up*) I'm going to lie down for a while. (*She walks
away, slowly, holding on to the furniture*)

ELENA: (*To* ANA) I'll make Beto's lunch, then I'll go. (*She removes
her rubber gloves*) Look at these hands, what a mess. I
was never beautiful, but I always had pretty hands. They
were the only thing I could ever brag about. I don't have
one decent fingernail. (*Pause*) Maybe Mario was right,
I should take care of myself. He has never been right
about anything in his life. I would like to think that he
was right this time, though. (*She chuckles*) It would be
a nice feeling. I'm not that old. Whom am I kidding?
(*She stares into the distance, and smiles*) Somebody must
like me. Maybe I should cut my hair. Maybe I should
start going out a little. It's been two years since Ralph
died. I don't want to end by myself. I need someone to
love. God, I have so much to give. (*She begins to run her
fingers through her hair*) I wonder what Ana would say if
she saw me with short hair. She'd probably die. Mario is
going to criticize me, of course, that's nothing new. What

do I care? I have had long hair all my life. It's part of
my personality. I'd probably look like a different woman.
That's not a bad idea! Hell, it's not too late! Yes, I think
I'll cut my hair. (*The lights begin to dim very slowly as she
plays with her hair. Blackout*)

WE INTERRUPT THIS PROGRAM ...

I can't do more than go my way
in this imaginary rumba.
The hips go here and there,
while the head, in rhythmic counterpoint,
is quite some years behind.
Stories forever told.
Worn-out formula
to be found in the wings of godlike children.
It's all been said before,
but hope feeds on its rebirth.
Patient Caribbean lion that I am,
stranded between four walls of summer's lament.
Sinner of sadness as Borges would have said.
Splendid vagabond among books
and women's photographs.
Abstract wanderer in the mythology
of a foreign tongue.
Violence that breathes by intuition
like a failing heart.
Divine game we all accept by now.
Departures and goodbyes we carry
with every shred of evidence.
Halfway between our lives and our deaths,
without wanting to die or to be born.
Tied up in total freedom,
always hoping for some gifts tomorrow will bring,
while we wear a heavy coat to hide the scars.

For each life a death,
early death I'm afraid.
We were all men last night.

What will become of us today?

I'll go on with yellowing books and falling hair;
on because there's no way
to go back to the beginning.
Once is enough perhaps, and yet,
how many of us would have desired a second chance.
There's no regret, only an ailing grin
for not having done better.

The women come, the woman I should say,
in furious repetition.
The woman I see in all females.
The one who has been with me all along.

The long, red fingernails,
a perfect pair of breasts,
the exhausting movement of her thighs.

The little girl, the wounded lady of despair,
the virgin sheets just in from the laundry.
Flesh of burning fire and roselike touch.
I am nothing but a man, animal and ageless child.
I am the world living in your silence,
in the mystery of a perfect night.
Unheard of melody, dancelike hours
in the eternity of your company.
Minutes and seconds of my days.
Men and women are all one,
the same now and forever.
I have nothing to give you but my song
and the currents from my river to carry your dreams.

There's a voice that keeps on coming from inside
while I build my days
from distant cries of childhood dreams:
A street, a house, a woman,
fading as she was with the country's agony on her face.
A voice from the dark that keeps on coming,
impersonal and straight as if it were a punching bag.
Yet, I must turn my face away,
not for fear of being hit
but just to keep on going.
In days like these, the word and the embrace

are born like a grasshopper's symphony.
He said, Heraclitus that is,
rivers are never the same.
River is a man that was and never again will be.
Distinctions we all reserve for a rainy day.
I had created worlds in the beginning,
long ago and far away,
when I was guardian of every human feeling,
carpenter of a perfect caress.
And yet, in spite of everything,
I must go on with my misgivings.

Smiles or tender seriousness
on faceless photographs.

The land I felt once mine has drifted into clouds.
Fragments remain, though, in recurrent souvenirs.
Sufferings that I have learned
only from the printed page.
Voices and faces almost alien, but not quite.
The rest is silence.

A NEW HEAVEN, A NEW EARTH

It had taken me almost two days to leave behind twenty years of vegetating among tropical flowers; two days of highway dancing from Miami to New York, during which I collected memories forgotten, words not said, emotions not felt, things not done. I went to New York not to find, but to forget; the city, however, had several surprises.

It was early morning as I left the Lincoln Tunnel. The sun, weaving its rays around Manhattan's skyscrapers, deciphered the city's echoes in lethargic innocence.

Estela, the niece of a deposed dictator from Central America, was my only acquaintance there. We had met in Miami, and had spent a weekend together. She was in her mid-thirties, with an eclectic look of a Mannerist portrait. About five-feet tall, and carrying 140 lbs. on her pseudo-Caribbean frame, she was not exactly a raving beauty. Young leftist radicals would look at her as a CIA parasite, a worm from the imperialist carcass. She had never questioned where her money came from: her dresses made in France, her American automobiles, her travels around the world, her lavish parties. She grew up without a care.

On Ninth Avenue, I stopped to phone her. Amazed and half asleep, she gave me her address, a three-story brownstone on Bank Street that her uncle had bought for her as a birthday present in the good-old-days. She had used the house for shopping trips to New York but, after the coup, there was no other alternative but to move there permanently. She lived with a girlfriend, a Newyorrican (Puertorrican New Yorker), whom she met while studying at Columbia University. Cyndie, the roommate, was a twenty-five-year-old tropical beauty who wanted to be loved for her brains.

She was the first beautiful, intelligent and completely liberated woman I ever met.

Estela insisted that I stay with them until I got settled. I had nowhere else to go, so I accepted.

My first day in New York was spent exorcising myself through a long and difficult narration of my life. That evening, both women already asleep, I found myself pacing up and down the spacious living room, whose walls were completely covered with paintings by Latin American artists. I lit a cigarette, and stood in front of the high window, looking out into the open mouth of night. I thought of that night when I was nine, and the growling, alcoholic voice of my father woke me up. He was shouting one obscenity after another. I went out into the hall and saw the enormous, wreckless hand of my father landing on my mother's delicate face. In a typical Spanish, Catholic, stoic manner, she was enduring the abuse for the sake of her children, because of what people would say, and because it wasn't expected of a "good" woman in Cuba to divorce her husband. My time travel also took me to the time when I was eighteen in Miami, and my father arrived home dead drunk. I was in the bedroom when I heard the commotion in the living room. I rushed out and saw my father, hardly standing on his feet, about to hit his helpless wife. I grabbed his heavy arm, while he cursed with all the strength his alcoholic lungs could muster. While holding him back, I pleaded with him, "Dad, stop. Dad, listen to me. I am your son, Dad." He couldn't hear, he couldn't think, he couldn't feel. He fell to the floor shouting, cursing. I was about to hit him, when I heard my mother's voice crying, "It's all right, son, it's all right. Don't, please; I can handle him."

Looking out the window of that New York apartment, my childhood seemed so far away, and yet, it was still so vivid in my mind! I never forgot any of it, I never wanted to forget. I kept on thinking about it in order not to forget, not a thing, not a single detail; my memories kept me alive.

I put out the cigarette and stood in the middle of Estela's living room; my right hand soared along the jungle of my long brown hair. I leaned against the backside of a corduroy sofa, and stared at a colored etching by Hernandez-Porto, "Rooster in Three Acts," in which the head, tail, and legs of a rooster had been separated and displaced over a surrealistic landscape of emerald green and sepia.

When I got up the following morning, Estela and Cyndie were gone; I had slept badly and very little. The bright summer sun bathed the living room, reminding me for a moment of Miami. No place is comforting when one is lonesome, when one has run out of escapes, like an ailing magician whose arthritis has vitiated his ability to do a sleight-of-hand trick, and who no longer possesses the confidence to saw a woman in half. My life had been held in suspended animation by my parents' decision to leave Cuba with Batista's downfall. No one really knew what was to happen, but they didn't have the curiosity to stay and find out; they packed their bags and left in a hurry, as the dictator had done, as the generals, the old-time politicians, the corrupt, the murderers had done; none of which they were. They took a plane and never looked back, relinquishing their home, their business, their clothes, their personal affairs, their love letters, their private moments, their childhood memories. Great changes were to take place in our country, and they would not be there to witness them, to participate in them. Why? I have always asked myself that question (I could never bring myself to ask them directly). "I always knew he (Fidel) was a communist. He never fooled me." That's how they rationalized the humiliating exodus, kidding themselves, of course. There weren't ten people in Cuba at the time who could tell a communist from a fascist; the only Marx they ever heard of was Groucho, and even him they didn't understand. Meanwhile, I was growing up in Miami with the painful feeling that I was an incomplete person. I couldn't stand their reactionary bragging, their loud cliches, their abject ignorance about what was happening to them and to their country. I understood them. I knew they needed to reminisce about the "paradise" that was Cuba in order to go on, to face each day, to begin anew, but I couldn't accept it, and I couldn't forgive them for dragging me along into their nostalgic carnival.

My parents were no different from other exiles; their sin was precisely in becoming exiles, and handing the country to someone whom they supposedly hated. Only a handful fought back; others stayed behind to see what they could get out of the new beginning, The have-nots of yesteryears wanted their piece of the pie. Millionaires aided Castro into power with the deranged notion that after his victory they would be able to get something out of it; Generals aided him—ordering soldiers not to fight the revolutionaries—deceiving themselves again; still they insisted on having known all along that Castro and company were communists. Fools. I despised them. I realized this that July morning in Estela's apartment. I had been fighting them by throwing my life away.

Then, there was Castro, the revolutionary leader, ideological misfit, fast gun, brother, father, lover, macho-extraordinaire of the New Cuba. All hated him and revered him. All males wanted to kill him, while trying to be like him; they mirrored his gestures, echoed his words, borrowed his demagoguery and envied him for living out all their fantasies. All females looked upon him as a respected father, a close friend, a movie star, a baseball player, their dream lover.

When each began to feel the true sting of the revolutionary bite, either by losing favors, possessions or a loved one, disenchantment showed its grimace.

Never again was I to see my hometown, my childhood friends, my cousins, and the grandmother who brought me up with a deluge of love, soft smiles and an always ready cup of light coffee, exceedingly sweet, to calm my ten-year-old tears. That morning in New York I understood myself, past and present, and I didn't like it.

I took a shower and decided to go out; it promised to be one of the hottest days of the young summer. Manhattan was devoid of the hustle and bustle of its daily living; it was almost desolate, except for taxicabs roaming around the city like gigantic yellow insects out of a Japanese science fiction movie. The streets were soft and steaming like freshly baked bread. The upper class had abandoned the city, the middle class made plans, the poor sweated it out along the streets, together with tourists.

I walked for hours with abandon, drifting along a river of self-esteem and self-disdain, turning in my mind all I remembered in an attempt to come to grips with myself. With elation and baseness, with trying movements, eyes gleaming, undulating hopes and a torrent of despair, I arrived at the Museum of Modern Art. I remembered the museum from previous trips to New York. Perfunctorily, I walked to the second floor galleries with their Cezannes and Matisses; I didn't stop to see any of my favorite paintings. Instead, I took the elevator to the sixth floor. Except for two women admiring a painting by Jasper Jones, the place was deserted. The restaurant was closed. I walked out into the terrace facing 53rd Street. With both hands, I grasped the top of the metal railing, and glanced at the street below; I had lost all sensation, the tips of my fingers white from the pressure of my grip. All of a sudden, I heard a voice, guttural, faint, but warm, with a certain note of immediacy about it: "I wouldn't do that." I turned around. Standing at the door was a short old man (he looked sixty-five or seventy), dressed in a dark blue suit. For a moment, I was stunned. Apparently, he thought that I was about to jump (the farthest thing from my mind), and he was trying to stop me. He was wearing dark glasses.

"I'm sorry," I said, "were you speaking to me?"

He seemed to realize his mistake, and added, "Oh, don't mind me."

"Who are you?" I asked.

"I'm no one," he answered immediately, and then added, "I'm just a blind old man. Blind to the sunlight, that is, where all pairs of opposites appear distinct." I didn't know what to make of that, then he went on, "I knew you were going to be here, in this very spot, exactly at this hour. You see, the gift of prophesy has the correlative vision of the inward eye, which penetrates the darkness of existence." Without giving me an opportunity to make a move, he extended his right hand (his left was holding a cane), and said, "Come, let's go down. Have you seen the Matisses they have here?" I looked at him with disbelief, but decided to play along; I thought the poor old man was nuts, so I would humor him for a while. He grabbed my arm and we went down. "Yes, yes, let's go see those beauties by the French master," he said with a friendly cast to his voice. "In Matisse a hand isn't simply a hand, but all the hands in the world; a body isn't simply the physical appearance of a human being, but a rhythmic accent from the symphony of life. The important thing in him is not the detail, but the total vision, the inner meaning of things. A human form, a line, color, are all unifying elements of an universal energy. Take a look over there," he said as we entered the second floor gallery, while pointing with his cane to one of the canvases. Still playing along like a fool, I walked over to the painting. After looking at it for a few seconds without any attempt to examine it, I turned around, but the old man had vanished. I felt emotionally stranded. How does a blind man know the work of Matisse? What was he doing in the museum? Who the hell was he? What did he want? I had no idea. I walked down the stairs and left.

I was succumbing to the notion that things were about to break loose. Had I been a religious man, I would have felt God's hand leading me along his chosen path. If I had only seen a sign, heard a voice. But I was nothing more than flesh and bones, and a mystical experience just wasn't in my stars.

Around seven-thirty, I got back to Estela's house; she, Cyndie and Antonio—her boyfriend—were drinking sangria, still in their swimsuits having just returned from the beach. Estela answered the door, took me by the hand and introduced me to the male guest.

"We went to the beach," she said after kissing me on the cheek. "You looked so tired, I didn't want to wake you." She handed me a glass of sangria as I lunged into an armchair.

"I've been walking around," I said after taking a long sip of the reddish concoction.

"My God! In this heat?" was her reaction. Then she went on, "Antonio has been telling us all about Americans in Cuba." He glanced at me, shrugged his shoulders and took a drag from his cigarette. He had a full moustache, and long, curly black hair, and was wearing dark glasses with a thin, black, metal frame. He was a chain smoker, and gesticulated constantly as he spoke in a vibrant baritone, the old macho, latin type, the lady killer. His eyes seemed to see through everything, a political fanatic, a promiscuous lover, street-wise, an all around tough guy that, even though he wasn't particularly handsome, was always attracted to beautiful women. He was everything I was not. "Listen, dear," Cyndie said to him, "why don't you continue your litany, now that you have another Cuban in the audience?" She was wearing a tiny, white bikini; her long, shapely legs seemed to fill the room; her slender, perfectly polished toes were still full of sand from the beach. I felt an ardent desire to caress her, to remove the sand from between her toes. She sneered at her boyfriend; it appeared to me that they loved each other, although they seemed to argue constantly about politics. She believed in the independence of Puerto Rico, her native land. *Independentistas*, as these young people were called, were moderate left-wingers, of different degrees; they were college graduates, and totally anti-American; the Cuban Revolution became their symbol for freedom, and that fact brought them face-to-face, on opposite sides of the political spectrum, with Cuban exiles. Yet, she was the girlfriend of one of them, and the sexual fantasy of another. She enjoyed getting Antonio's goat. I don't know why, possibly for my art, but I always seem to be attracted to women I can't have. I've been either unlucky, or a fool; perhaps both.

"I was just telling them how Americans have always been sticking their heads where they're not invited." Antonio's voice startled me. I was nudged by the tone of his voice; he seemed to put his whole being into each word; each phrase was an affirmation, he never hesitated. "During our War of Independence," he continued, "the Americans wanted Cuba to abandon Spain and join the Union; it was all on account of the slaves and the money." I was too drained to get involved in the conversation; instead, I was imagining making love to Cyndie, with her long legs wrapped around my waist. During my sexual daydreaming, I caught tidbits of the young man's pugnacious monologue. Estela was sitting on the floor, next to me; she had placed her arm over mine; with her eyes gleaming and her skin half-burned, she was relishing the whole affair. I glanced at her with what must have been a pitiful smile; I thought that it would be easy for her to fall in love with me, but I also knew that I would never reciprocate. I could have been her friend, her lover, but nothing else. Meanwhile, Antonio rambled on, "Had we gone along with them, we would all be wearing cowboy hats in the Caribbean. Jefferson, with all his Architecture and his Democracy, was the first to open the door. Polk followed suit, and in 1857 Buchanan was still attempting to buy us, all in the name of Liberty. Thank God for Republicans!"

Cyndie snapped at him, "All you Cubans are stupid, you know?"

"Sure," he exclaimed, "had we been talking about Puerto Rico, it would have been a different story, no?"

"It might have been refreshing!" she replied.

Enjoying the mordant give-and-take between the two lovers, I couldn't take sides; I just sat in awe of that beautiful woman with a command of historical facts and convictions that would have put a politician to shame. I must admit that I had succumbed overnight to her charms. They continued to rip each other's arguments apart, he as the right-wing revolutionary, she as the liberal luminary. It all ended with a laugh and a hug, but neither had given any ground. There was an underside to that incident; the two lovers arguing about politics left a mark on me. I had been a philistine, living on the periphery of my convictions about Cuba. I had dogged the issue, but it was in vain. Cuba was embedded in me; I had to harvest my involvement anew. Cyndie, with her long legs, and Antonio, with his flowing moustache, had stultified me that evening, but I was not ashamed. I knew then I was on the right track. Before leaving, Antonio invited me for lunch the following Monday; I agreed. Cyndie went to take a shower; Estela picked up the glasses and went into the kitchen. I walked to the table, picked up my notebook and read: " ... neither do we live completely for ourselves but, in great part, for others; not always for our own well-being, but for another's, and for the happiness of others."

ANTONIO'S RAINBOW

I met Antonio the following Monday, as I had agreed to do, at a Cuban-Chinese restaurant on West 14th Street. When I arrived, he was standing by a table near the window facing the street; a newspaper was laid open on the table, not as if it was being read, but more as if it was being displayed—for its virtues or its vices— awaiting someone's subjectively passionate criteria. The printed words and images from the paper in question had taken a new meaning, a new personality, a new dimension on the sleazy July afternoon. Antonio, the director of a Spanish language newspaper himself, was showing off the professional look of the *Diario de las Americas*. This happened to be the same paper for which I used to write film and drama criticism in Miami. It was the social page he had been praising. "Look at this picture," I heard him say, "all pretty faces; there isn't an ugly person there. I don't want to be nasty, but the damn people we get in Washington Heights can scare a child to death."

I approached the table; his handshake and wide smile greeted me with the familiarity of a lifelong friend. "Nice to see you," he said, gesturing for me to take a sit across the table from him. "I have been showing these Chinese what a newspaper should look like." The Chinese were the waiters, all relatives, Cuban-Chinese, most of them formerly from Canton, who had gone to Cuba seeking a better life. After Castro they continued their search for the good life in the U.S., opening a chain of restaurants. New York became a paradise for such entrepreneurs; 8th Avenue, 23rd Street and 14th Street were all fertile grounds for their food empires (once they ventured to Lexington Avenue, but it was a flop). Their restaurants were simple, cheap, and the food came in large portions: yellow rice, chicken with yellow sauce, yellow custard; a preponderance of yellow overwhelmed the menu, juxtaposing the reddish-orange

decor—mostly out of plastic—with all sorts of green ornamenta-
tion dangling from every inch of open space on the greasy ceiling.
The menu was listed in Spanish, while most of the clientele was
composed of young, poor Americans; however, the orders were
called out to the cook in Chinese. Antonio looked nervous. He was
smoking, drinking coffee, and talking his head off—which I found
out later on were his trademarks—his moustache was filtering every word, his eyes danced with every syllable. He was impeccably
dressed as always. Antonio Perez-Perez, a Cuban playboy, a bright
journalist, and an ardent revolutionary; he was continuing a long
tradition of Cuban men of action. He was, as one would expect,
an exceptional conversationalist who was loved by everyone who
knew him.

"Yes sir, this is really something," he sounded off. "I tell you.
One really has to put up with lots of shit in this world. What the
hell, this is *Le plus mieux des mondes possible*; if it isn't, we've
really been taken. After 15,000 years of history, I wind up on 14th
Street, a fourth class market-place where you can buy anything on
sale and on credit. There's no evil that won't bring some good
sooner or later. No sir, all the saints, sporting flashy-colored out-
fits and their showbiz smiles, are neatly stacked in a botanica's display window offering protection and hope. Seashells on tabletops,
and greasy hands from downtown factories grab onto the handles
of the IRT, Jerome bound, while their tropical feeling spills over
Manhattan."

As I sat opposite him, a young blond girl, wearing tight shorts,
walked by; Antonio rushed to the door and shouted, "Honey, listen, you do something to me, you know? I'm melting for you.
Look at me, don't be mean; I have it in for you, baby, whenever
you want it. C'mon, sugar pie, don't leave me." Turning to me, he
said, "So much meat walking around, and I am starving." When
it came to sex he certainly wasn't starving; for one, there was Cyndie, the Puertorrican woman of my dreams, and God knows how
many more. He folded the newspaper, and called the waiter: "Oye,
Mario, give me two Millers and the menu. Make sure it's cold; not
the menu, but the beer." He sat down and continued, "It's hot as
hell out there; a great day for the beach, this damn 14th Street is
an oven." With a flowing movement of his hand, he pointed to
the window, "Shit, look at that police car." Another girl passed
by, again he shouted through the glass; then he looked at me, grin-
ning. "You know," he said, "one of these days I'm gonna bite one
of those chicks; they walk around showing off everything, no bra,
no nothing."

"It's tempting," I said, to which he replied, "I get hungry just by looking." The waiter came with the two beers and the menu, stained with black bean soup, beef stew sauce, and clouds of vinegar and oil; all in a Pollockian arrangement of memories of former dinners.

"Thank you, Mario," Antonio said to the waiter. "These Chinese are tops. You see this guy? Three times he tried to escape from Cuba, and three times he was caught. Tell him about it, Mario."

Apparently the waiter was used to Antonio's routine, although he seemed quite eager to tell me the story. "The first time that I tried to escape was by boat," he began, while standing at our table. "Two friends of mine and myself began to build this boat by night. We had to build one because there was no way we could steal one. The militia men watched closely everything that could float; we had to build it at night because we worked all day long. So, in an extra room we had in my house, we started building the boat. We finished it, and we made all the preparations for our escape. We said goodbye to our mother, we took some food, and we waited until the whole town was asleep; then we picked the boat and started for the door. Do you know what happened? We couldn't get the boat through the door, it was too big. We had spent over two months building the damn boat and we never bothered to measure it."

"You're a disgrace to the Chinese people," Antonio said to him, poking fun.

The waiter, indifferent to Antonio's remarks, went on. "It happens; we were so involved with our dreams that we didn't think the boat had to fit through the door. We tried again, though; we weren't gonna be discouraged. Instead of building another boat, which took too long, we decided to build a raft. With some effort we were able to get four tire tubes, and with several wood planks we made it; we had a sail, and for protection we made a huge kite to give us more speed. A few weeks after the first attempt, we took to sea on our raft; we were doing fine, the wind was taking us away from the coast, and all of a sudden, the direction of the wind changed. Instead of moving away from the coast, it began to take us in again. We didn't want to let go of the kite, because we were afraid of being stranded in the middle of the ocean, so we went back. But we were determined to leave, so we had to try once again. The third time we got more daring, we stole a small boat. In the middle of the night, as we had done before, we left Matanzas, rowing like wild men until we finally lost sight of the bay. The following morning we saw land once again; boy, we were so happy! We had made this big banner that said, 'Thank you, America!' As we began to approach the coast, we took out our banner, and began to shout, 'Thank you, American; Thank you, America.' We thought we were in Key West or Miami, instead we had arrived at Havana. They gave us ten years in jail."

Antonio—even though he had heard the story many times before—was cracking up. "Didn't I tell you the Chinese were tops?"

"It was fun," the waiter said philosophically, then he asked, "What you wanna eat?"

Antonio ordered for both of us, assuring me he knew the menu by heart, and that I should trust his judgement. He looked out the window again, as he took a sip from his beer. "Yeah, 8th Avenue and 14th Street. Beer cans grow on these streets like tulips in Holland." He poured some more beer into my glass, and announced, "Because when you feel like having more than one, I feel like having more than one, and it ain't a Schaefer." He looked at the window once again, and exclaimed, "What an ass, goddamit. These American women are something else. To think that when I came to this country, everyone told me that American women were cold. Boy, were they wrong." He remained pensive for a while, his face changed, his moustache dropped. For the first time, I saw him very serious; then he took a sip from his beer. "You know," he said, "I know your work. I have read some of your articles, I've read some of your poems. We need people like you. I would like you to come to one of our meetings. We're doing little things, quietly, but steady." The food came. "Do you have any plans?" he asked.

"No, I have to get settled first, I just got here. Eventually I would like to do some writing. I have done some research on Martí, I would like to write a play about him."

"Martí? No kidding?"

"I have been working on it for some time now."

"You know, I direct a newspaper here. If you want, you can write about theater and so on." Then he took something out of his mouth. "This tastes like shit." He called out to the waiter, "Mario, what the hell is this? It tastes like dirt with ketchup." Then he turned to me, "I'm telling you, Columbus thought he had discovered a paradise: 'a happy land, without sickness, without old or death, without fear'. He really missed the boat."

"When did you leave Cuba?" I asked him.

"Sixty-two." Then he called to the waiter, "Mario, two coffees."

"Why did you leave?"

"That son-of-a-bitch turned communist on us."

"Do you think so?"

"What do you mean?"

"Do you think he was a communist all along," I asked, "or do you think he turned communist afterwards?"

"I don't think he was anything before. As a student he was nothing more than an empty-headed gangster."

"Why do you think that he has stayed in power for so long?" I asked, observing how the blood began to boil in his veins. Cuba was a subject—I soon found out—that dominated his existence.

"In 1959," he began, marking each word, "everyone in Cuba was euphoric with the triumph of the Revolution; we were all for it, we wanted to make it work. We thought that we would become the first really free country in Latin America, independent of the United States." He lit a cigarette and took a deep drag, then he said meticulously, "The Platt Amendment and the Monroe Doctrine were two wounds inflicted on us by the Americans, for which we can never forgive them. They robbed us of our self-determination. They robbed our soldiers in the War of Independence of their right to win or lose their liberty; Americans made us incomplete men, they made us into a politically crippled society that was dependent on the United States for its social stability." He leaned back in his chair, took a deep breath, and continued, "Castro got rid of the Americans for us, but look where he got us. Cuba isn't socialist or communist, it's a capitalist dictatorship associated with the Russians. We just don't learn, brother. That's why we need men like you."

"I don't know, I'm not much of a revolutionary."

"Nobody's anything until circumstances force them to become something."

"Perhaps I never found myself in such a situation," I said with a bit of sarcasm.

"Don't worry," Antonio said while exhaling a curtain of smoke between us, "you will."

We were both trying to feel each other out: he was doing it for political reasons, he wanted to see if I could be useful to their cause; I was doing it for personal reasons, I wanted to know what kind of people they were, those anti-Castro revolutionaries. He was trying to put me on the spot, something that I had always resisted; I don't like to be used, I don't like to be forced into situations of which I am not in control. I realized that I was very cynical then and very condescending. At times I felt very close to him, other times I felt I came from another planet. What was there about those young Cuban exiles that kept them so involved with the politics of their country? Some of them had left their homeland as small children, and still they felt for that small island as if they had never left it. I could understand the older generation being attached to their country, their past; but those young people had had no past there; so, what pulled them towards that myth of a country had to be a feeling. It was nothing tangible or tactile; it was a nostalgic longing for something they never had, but wished they had had; it was a life they had been robbed of, even if that life was worse than the one they were living in the United States. Antonio had left Cuba in 1962, by boat, with his family and some friends. In 1961, at the age of 16, he had been arrested during the Bay of Pigs invasion; he was one of over half a million people suspected of subversive activities that had been arrested in less than forty-eight hours. He had studied history at New York University, where he debated his way—and sometimes fought his way—through four years with left-wing professors and student members of the SDS. He had made a name for himself as a hardheaded anti-Castro activist; he wrote against the Castro regime every day, and denounced it at every political rally he attended. He made the Cuban cause his cause; he lived it and eventually died for it. Cuban men have always known how to die for their country, but few have known how to live for it.

After a long pause, Antonio spoke again. "One cannot live on the periphery of things."

I looked him in the eye. When he saw that I was not going to answer, he continued, "Most of the time we live for no meaningful reasons. It's better to live for a wrong reason than for no reason at all." He lit another cigarette and took a sip from his cold coffee. "You know," he continued, "Camus used to say that without the memory of a lost home or a promised land, man is an exile without remedy; I am an exile, but I have a remedy, I have a reason." I felt like asking him what the hell was all the sermon about; I felt like telling him to save his rhetoric for his readers and his right-wing friends, but he was a likable guy, and besides, he had invited me to lunch. Instead, I heard myself saying, "I wish I had a reason."

"Things will fall into place. You've been away too long, brother, it's time you got back."

"I have been living a death with nothing else following it," I said, quoting Kierkegaard.

"One is always a prisoner of one's own truths. The devil is in the Bronx, my friend, in Manhattan, in China, in Cuba. He is in us, in our actions, in our words. One has to fight him constantly. One way of fighting is by being useful. by making our lives mean something."

He thought that he had me then; he thought I was falling for all his bull.

"What do you want me to do," I asked sarcastically, "become a member of Omega 7?"

"You don't have to become a member of anything. You're not American, or Greek, or Armenian. You're Cuban, for better or worse."

"That much I know."

"We have lots of things to talk about," he said, putting out his cigarette. He glanced at his watch, picked up his newspaper, put on his sunglasses, fixed the collar of his shirt and looked out the window. He shook my hand and said, "I have to go; I'm glad we got together, I'm glad you're here; you're on your way. I am going to set up that job for you in the newspaper, okay? I'll call you at Estela's."

"Okay."

"There isn't much money in it, but it's something. It will get you started anyway."

"Don't worry about it. I'll take care of the check, you go on ahead."

I watched him as he walked across the street to his car. I ordered another cup of espresso, and stared out the window, through the sign with red letters that spelled out backwards, EL PARAISO RESTAURANT.

2

I was born in Victoria de las Tunas, a little town in the province of Oriente. By the time I was three, my family had moved to an even smaller town, Puerto Padre; it was a seaport where there were no fishermen, or very few anyway. My father had been offered a job to take charge of a lumberyard in Puerto Padre by his employer in Tunas. The owners of the lumberyard came from a wealthy family, of which several members were involved in national politics. Since politics in Cuba was a matter of friendship, it would come in handy in the future when my family needed a favor, but it seems that it also proved to be a liability when the Batista government fell. The lumberyard wasn't much to speak of, but it offered an adequate income for the growing family. As a matter of fact, it made us members of the little town's "High Society." My grandparents continued to live in Tunas. We used to visit them often. My grandfather, on my mother's side, was a little man from northern Spain who worked for the railroad. He worked for six months, or during *La Zafra*—the time it took to harvest the sugar cane—laying down railroad tracks. The following six months were those of *tiempo muerto*, the "dead time," during which there was nothing to do for most people. For six months they had food and money and some new clothes. When my brother and I went to visit them, we used to go to a neighbor's house at night where, for a penny, we were allowed to watch television for about two hours. Popcorn and candy was an extra cent. When the *tiempo muerto* came, money ran out, and they had to buy everything on credit, including groceries. With a small notebook, I would go to the store to buy three cents of sugar or five cents of lard. Sometimes for lunch there was nothing more than sweet potatoes mashed with warm lard and a glass of water. I remember looking out the kitchen window, and seeing my cousin Miguelito, who was about four or five, walk to the back of the house and squat, defecating an interminable swarm of thin, whitish tapeworms; then he would get up and go back to playing. From that type of life, my brother and I would return to Puerto Padre in our white linen suits from Ireland. We grew up among hunger and riches, among sickness, drunkards, lost women, and the comfortable life of a prosperous family with powerful friends. By 1957, while people in Havana were dancing their lives away, in Oriente there were daily shootings in the streets, sometimes forcing eighteen to sleep on the floor in order to escape the bullets fired at random against the houses, either by scared soldiers, by students doing acts of sabotage, or by a group of revolutionaries that had come down from the mountains nearby. By October of 1958, my father had left the country; he had lost his business, I never knew how or why. My brother and I stayed behind with our mother who had to begin working to support us; she drove a delivery truck for a bakery. Sometimes she would come home at two or three in the morning; I never heard her complain, though. Then she became ill and could no longer drive the truck. My father could not send us any money from the United States. So, she turned to his former employers. They would give her a few dollars here and there. She was begging for us, without humiliating herself ever. When the national elections came around, one of the sons of the Rosa family who was running for representative came around to collect my mother's voting book; one favor was paid with another. Finally the visa came, and we joined our father in Miami. On that day, Batista and his comrades left the island in the hands of the revolutionaries still in the mountains. All that the former leaders of our country wanted to do was to take their suitcases full of dollars out of the country.

There I was on that July afternoon in a cheap restaurant on 14th Street, such a long way from Puerto Padre. Yet, I really had gone nowhere. I just heard words, I just felt words, in an endless repetition: a silence shared, born into, walked over, eaten together with three meals a day. Twenty words in twenty years was my conversation with my father, a cry of anguish, a helplessness, unimportant arrivals and departures. If we only had the strength to admit that we need others to help us.

"Eight twenty-five," the waiter said, handing me the check. I gave him a ten dollar bill and went outside. When I got to the sidewalk, the same girl from before passed by me, going in the opposite direction this time; she looked at me and smiled—with a carefree, half innocent, half tempting disregard—as only an American woman can.

Through one of her friends, Estela got me an apartment on East 87th Street, where I managed to survive the month of July without air conditioning. By the beginning of August, I caught up with New York's cultural explosion; the press pass from Antonio's newspaper, *Última Hora,* was no small help. Estela and I saw each other on and off; our relationship was slowly becoming a good friendship. Cyndie was wearing out as a fantasy; Antonio and I had by then become close friends, so that was that. For the first time in many years, there wasn't a woman in my life.

Once a week Antonio succeeded in dragging me to a meeting of his revolutionary group, which took place in the basement of a travel agency in Union City, New Jersey. I remember one in particular: Antonio and I were late as usual; he could never bring himself to be punctual. The discussion was in full force when we got there; hell had broken loose among the anti-Castro faithful, twenty or thirty people were screaming their heads off simultaneously. Through the cursing and shouting we said hello, shook hands and took our place against the back wall. The night before, two members of the group had been arrested while attempting to place a bomb at the Cuban Mission to the United Nations. Apparently, someone had tipped-off the FBI: there was a traitor in the group, they had been infiltrated, they were not as united as they had thought they were; in their most private refuge they were still prey to either Castro or the Americans; in the only ambition that remained to them—to liberate their country—they could not even pretend to exercise their right as free men without some outside interference. The question of how or why it happened would have to wait for another time; however, what was more pressing was to get the two boys—they were eighteen and twenty respectively—out of jail. The commotion at that meeting was of trying to decide how to raise the bail money; someone suggested a dinner party at fifty dollars a plate; someone else suggested a dance—Cubans would pay anything to help the cause if they could dance. While a short old man banged his fists against the podium and exhorted his compatriots, not to take the easy way out. Cubans, he insisted, must help the cause of freedom with any sacrifice necessary. Liberty didn't come easy, and everyone had to do his or her share. It was time, he continued, to stop dancing and having dinners, and think more seriously about their homeland, held in chains. There were cries of assent that carried a long history of suffering, an acuteness of pain; the eyes of most of those grown men and women were filled with tears, not perhaps because of the two young men being held in a New York jail, but because that incident, like many others, brought home to them the certainty of their displacement, the pain of their not belonging, the agonizing feeling of not even having one's own place to do one's own suffering.

A tall mulatto who seemed to be one of the leaders tried in vain to calm the old man. "We agree with you, Francisco, we agree; we'll do whatever is necessary; don't worry, we'll take care of the money. Leave it to us, Francisco, leave it to us."

The meeting broke up, and for about two hours after that, the discussion went on. I couldn't feel what they felt, and for the first time in my life I realized that I was worse off for not being able to agonize with them, but I just didn't, and I couldn't change that. I never participated in any of their discussions, but I had listened intensely to their ideology and their plans; they had faith, they were dedicated, they lived with the eternal hope of returning, with the eternal longing for the past, that was their sin. They were right-wing in their political thinking because the left had taken over their places; they abhorred communism because it had stripped them of all they had known as a normal way of life. Given the right circumstances they could, perhaps, be more liberal than any man, more progressive than any man, but not as exiles, not as pariahs.

The following day, I received a letter from Miami. As he often did, Lalo had written to keep me up-to-date on the life in the Cuban exile capital. Rolando Lima had had a stroke; one side of his body became totally paralyzed—his former wife still helped him with the laundry and the cooking, but she would not go back to live with him, so he was taken to a state-run nursing home. The other member of our old quintet, Aldo, had disappeared; there was speculation that he had landed in Cuba with two other men in some sort of a commando raid: they were smuggling arms into the island in an attempt to repeat Castro's feat of getting to the mountains and waging war against the government. Miami and its inhabitants never reached out beyond their own private world.

To my surprise and delight, my poetry was rather well known to literary minded Cubans living in New York; I had become—through no fault of my own—one of the few poets who was admired by his compatriots in and out of the island at the same time. That was a dangerous situation, as I would later find out; they all coveted my position, but hated me for it.

On October 10th, to commemorate a Cuban national holiday—the beginning of the War of Independence in 1868—I was invited to give a poetry reading at Hunter College. The United Cuban Student Organization, as my hosts were called, was a group of politically minded young Cubans who for the most part studied political science and Spanish literature. To satisfy them, I selected my strongest poems—politically speaking—although they were not my best, but they fitted the bill. The reading turned out to be a modest success; I had managed to impress them, using my acting abilities to dramatize each poem. The interesting part of the event was not my reading, however, but the people I met there: Ariadne Lopez, a philosophy student with the body of a Las Vegas showgirl came up to me with a somber look on her face, looked me in the eye, and said, "I like your poetry very much, thank you for coming." And that was that; with the swiftness with which she arrived, she turned around and left. She didn't give me a chance to react, to ask for her telephone number, to try to be charming, to invite her to lunch, to give her one of my hooks, nothing; she left me with my mouth open and an air of dejection on my face.

Leonardo Caturla, a young political science professor at the college who was working on his Ph.D. thesis shook my hand very firmly and said, "Atta boy! That's the way to do it; I'd like to talk to you some time. Here is my number, call me when you can."

"Yes," I said. "Sure I will call you."

Then he introduced a bearded man who was with him; we shook hands, and then he took out a small notebook, wrote something in it and handed it to me. It read, "Congratulations. Have you read Huang Po?"

"No," I said to him, a bit mystified; then he wrote again in his notebook and handed me the piece of paper, "We have lots of thing to talk about."

That one really got me; Leonardo Caturla noticed the puzzled look on my face, and explained, "Osvaldo is not speaking now."

"Oh," I said. Then he wrote again, "Words are not important."

To a guy that had just given a poetry reading, that was no small insult.

"You're right," I said trying to be funny. He wrote once more in his notebook and handed me the paper—by then I had a collection of scraps of paper in my hand. It read, "Osvaldo Fernandez, this is my number, call me." We all shook hands, they departed, and I looked all over the room for the philosopher with the showgirl's body to no avail. The day ended with a disconcerted feeling: Who were all those people I had just met? They fascinated me, they intrigued me; and I intended to find out, to study them, to find myself through them.

Two days later she called; she, the showgirl-philosopher, Ariadne Lopez, the sober-minded beauty from my poetry reading. As it turned out, she was a friend of Antonio, my journalist-revolutionary friend; he had given her my telephone number. There was to be a political rally in Union City, New Jersey, and she wanted to know if I would speak to an expected group of about two thousand Cubans, who would gather there. I didn't think a political rally was an adequate place to talk about poetry, so I didn't consider myself a good candidate for the occasion; I told her as much, but she was determined to get me there. Most of the speakers were going to be old time revolutionaries and political cronies. Ariadne was desperately trying to get a new face to appear at the rally that would appeal to the young Cubans in the audience. She suggested I speak about Martí; Antonio had told her I was an authority on the subject. I wasn't an authority on José Martí, but I couldn't back down; I did tell Antonio about my involvement with Martí, besides, I wanted to see her again if it meant speaking at a political rally, I would have to acquiesce. I accepted. The day of the rally was a Sunday afternoon; it was to take place in a baseball stadium. I thought the whole thing a bit surrealistic; instead of speaking about Martí, I decided to use part of one of his own speeches—about a hundred years old—to deliver to the politically-minded sports fans in New Jersey. I didn't tell any one my little joke. Antonio was going to drive me there; as usual, we were late. After parking our car, it took us about half an hour to get to the park: every twenty feet he would stop to greet someone, like a politician the night before the elections, like a baseball player after a good game. It was late afternoon when we finally entered the park; the stands were packed: Cubans of all ages had gathered there to hear speeches they had already heard many times before, to see the people they saw every day, to express the anguish and frustration they expressed every hour of their lives. It was like the

World Series of Anti-Castro politics: political leaders, community leaders, business leaders, radio personalities, well-known pre-1959 actors, aging television stars. Everyone was there, including students, babies, old people. Refreshments were being sold, as well as banners, poetry books and revolutionary manifestos. At second base they had built a stage about four feet high, with a huge Cuban flag as a backdrop. When we arrived, there was a young man singing, accompanying himself with a guitar, while someone held a microphone near his mouth; past home plate you couldn't hear a thing. In the stands people were carrying on as if the events had not yet started. The pleasure of Cuban conversation! In a Cuban you will find charm and friendship; when you have two Cubans, there is good conversation and laughter; with three Cubans you have chaos on your hands. With two thousand Cubans, well ... At third base, two women in their sixties, carried a large banner which read, DOWN WITH TYRANNY. Someone shouted, "¡Viva Cuba Libre!" and the crowd responded with a deafening "¡Que Viva!" without realizing that the poor folk singer was still pouring his heart out on second base. Finally, someone on the dais noticed that the microphones were not working. "What do you mean, not working?" one of the leaders asked. "Oh, shit! Sabotage." After a chaotic half hour they got the sound going. The speeches—another Cuban specialty—began; no one can talk longer than a Cuban with a microphone; Castro, of course, was the prime example. Castro had already announced that he was going to free the political prisoners, thus making that subject the least mentioned in the rally; but they spoke of just about everything else. They all began with something like, "The vile tyrant ... " "Our homeland in chains ... ," or, "The beast that governs our country ... "

Finally my turn at the microphone came. I had never before spoken from second base, in front of two thousand people, not even when playing ball—I had always played left field in my youth. Most of the people gathered at the baseball park had no idea who the hell I was; it took a long introduction to justify my presence amongst them. I wasn't sure that the master of ceremonies had succeeded; he was a radio announcer, and his flowery introduction in a deep, echoing voice seemed to have gotten lost in that huge park like a misdirected foul ball. They gave me their attention just the same, or at least the same amount of attention they had given everyone else that preceded me. I said some brief introductory words and began my impersonation of José Martí:

"When the sun shines for everyone, except for us, when the snow cheers everyone except us, when for everyone except for us

Nature has changes and different fragrances, a soft breeze comes from the sea, moaning, to speak to us about hardships that haven't yet found relief; of human beings that disappear in the middle of the night, of mutilated rights—sometimes even harder to accept than the dead men and women—; thus we live."

For the first time during the whole afternoon there was total silence in the stadium; my words—Martí's words—bounced against the stands, the outfield walls, the banners, like an improbable proclamation. As I spoke I was hearing myself for the first time, stressing strong accents on the consonants, and eternally elongating the vowels. I was captivating the crowd and confusing myself. Did I begin at that moment to believe what I was saying? I don't know; I continued.

"Who amongst us here is not aware of how we live? We don't want to go back. As cruel as this life of ours is, life there is crueler."

I realized that the words I was saying were said a hundred years before, and they had not lost their meaning nor their truth; life in our country had not changed much. I took a long pause to look at the crowd, then continued.

"War brought us here, and our hatred for tyranny keeps us here; a hatred so rooted in us, so essential to our nature. Why should we return, when it isn't possible to live there with decorum, and the time to die has not yet arrived? Go there, for what? To see our brothers oppressed, living in silence and chains? To see a whole country, our country, living in shame and in fear? A knife wound is not enough to say how much it hurts. Others may go back, we cannot."

I finished speaking, and for a few moments time stood still, hearts stood still. Not because of me, of course, but because through the words of the "finest man the island of Cuba has given to the world," I had opened the deepest wound in them. At that time Castro had allowed members of the Cuban exile community to go back and visit their relatives in the island; not because of humanitarian reasons, but because he needed the American dollars they would take to spend there. Whether to return or not, under the conditions outlined by Castro, was dividing the exiles; without knowing this I had chosen the words that made the questioning of their dilemma that much more caustic. Finally someone shouted, "*¡Viva Cuba Libre!*" and the whole stadium responded, "*¡Que Viva!*" It seemed like all of New Jersey was embracing me; some women (probably mothers of political prisoners) cried on my shoulders. "We are proud of having young people like you. I wish my children had been here. With so much corruption in the world, it's refreshing to see young men like you." I don't have to tell you that I felt like two cents, my little joke had backfired on me. For days on end my phone didn't stop ringing. All anti-Castro organizations wanted me to give a speech at some meeting.

A few days after my baseball park performance I received a telephone call from the old man I met at the Museum of Modern Art on that strange afternoon. Marcos—as he called himself—wanted me to meet him that evening at the Cats of the West, a little club on the west side. Without waiting for a reply, he hung up.

Too many inexplicable things had been happening to me during those two months in New York; I even wondered whether Luis Vega was correct in his prediction that I had a mission, but I couldn't bring myself to really fall for that. It was romantic, but my vanity didn't carry me that far. I couldn't rationalize any of it, so I simply opted for taking one thing at a time; my only reaction was to wait and see. I felt a certain curiosity about the old man, I was itching to find out who the hell he was: a blind man, in a museum, trying to stop me from committing suicide? I couldn't resist! So I went that evening to the Cats of the West.

Down some ten steps and through a narrow glass door I entered the bar. There were ten or twelve men gathered near the door, inspecting the newcomers, visually savoring the newcomers, tempting the newcomers: I had entered a gay club. I was about to walk out, when I caught a glance of the old man, Marcos, sitting at a table in the back. He was wearing the same dark blue suit as when I met him at the museum, his "Ceremonial Blue Suit," as Eugenio Florit had said of Langton Hughes. As I approached the table he smiled and asked me to sit down.

"How are you, my son?" he asked, like a grandfather, with a relaxed tone of voice, then he added, "I'm glad you came."

"You are not blind, are you?" I asked almost immediately after sitting opposite him.

"No," he answered, "it was a necessary disguise."

The waiter, a young man in his twenties, came to take the order for drinks.

"Life is not simple," he continued, "the world is in a mess; and there's nothing we can do about it; we must offer our contribution and hope for the best." He took a sip from his drink, took a deep breath, and continued. "All right, let's get down to basics. We have been following you for some time now."

"Why?" I asked.

"Since Miami," he said, and looked at me intensely, like a father about to make a great revelation to his son. Then he placed both hands on the table, and leaned forward. Almost whispering, he confessed, "I work for the Cuban government." I must have turned white; my hands began to perspire. The old man leaned back in his seat, with an apparent air of satisfaction on his face; he was pleased with my reaction. The disco music that had been playing all along seemed to me to have intensified. "Don't be shocked," he continued, there are many like me here, in New York. Listen, son, we live under difficult times; before we spoke to you, we had to be sure of who and what you were. You understand?"

"No, I don't understand."

"Son, we have been in power for twenty years now. The Revolution is irreversible; forget what the exiles say, we have things under control. Believe me, no one is going to overthrow our government from the outside."

He had lowered his voice to a point where I could hardly make out his words. He looked me in the eye, while puffing on his cigarette; then he continued, "As you know, we have allowed the exiles to return to the island to visit their families. We are releasing the political prisoners, and there have been quite a few cultural exchanges. Of course, we haven't allowed any of our foes to re-enter the country; fools we're not." He paused for a while, and remained pensive; he was studying me. Then he started again, "I'm gonna be frank with you, I don't have long to live. Before you were born I was already fighting repressive governments in our country. In all my years I have never been able to see our country united for anything, except in 1959; then we were united. That was a glorious year for us, but it didn't last."

His words came to me from behind a curtain of smoke in an slow, deliberate tone. "There are those who say that the Revolution was betrayed. Sour grapes! There was no other way out for us, we had to be radical; we had to start from scratch. As it was to be expected, we made mistakes, we were new at the game of running a country. Boy, did we make mistakes! We began growing tomatoes in rice fields; we slaughtered bulls that we should have kept for breeding; all the professionals and the technicians had left the country; there wasn't a damn revolutionary that knew a thing about anything. Our primary concern was survival—political survival— latter on we would learn how to grow tomatoes. Everything went wrong for us: our sugar harvests failed to produce the record crops we had hoped for; our society failed to create the "new man" out of our new reality; our leaders failed to motivate our workers with moral incentives—there were no material incentives to give; but in spite of it all, we stayed in power."

"How about all of those you sent to the firing squads?" I asked, not pretending to be the devil's advocate, but simply trying to get my head together.

"That was necessary," he said, leaning back in his chair, "we had to eliminate the opposition, you can understand that. Had you been in power, you would have done the same."

"But you destroyed a whole way of life."

"There was no time for inventory."

"Maybe there was no time, but did anyone care?"

The music stopped; the bartender announced through a microphone, "In a few minutes, showtime."

The old man finished his drink and ordered another—I had yet to touch mine—and then he said with sarcasm, "You haven't been an exemplary exile yourself; all you do is criticize them, you're not one of them."

There was a great deal of truth in that, but I wasn't about to give him the satisfaction of admitting it.

"I'm not one of you either," I said.

"That's the point!" he exclaimed. "You're the perfect man, you are neutral, you are an intellectual ... "

A trio of musicians began playing; the bartender, in a very high-pitched voice, announced, "Here she is once again, the sensation of New York's night life, let's welcome her with all we have to offer, "la Traviata."

The small lounge had rapidly filled since my arrival; the audience —ninety-eight percent male—applauded and cheered, and whistled. "La Traviata" had nothing to do with Verdi's opera; it or she was a travesty who used to close her show with a parody of an aria from the Italian masterpiece. She was about six feet tall, and wore a bright red dress, paved with rhinestones, right out of a *fin-de-siecle* salon in Paris, which was very becoming to what looked like her "natural" breasts. Her make-up, realistic and quite toned down, made her look as beautiful as any woman on Fifth Avenue. The show went from classical to popular to down right raunchy. The audience frenetically asked for one encore after another; at each turn, La Traviata bowed elegantly, with all the grace that her large frame could muster. Offering incessant thank you's in an imperceptible tone of voice, she hurriedly left the tiny stage.

"Will you please come with me," the old man said, while getting up. I was torn between going with him, telling him to go to hell, or just leaving the homosexual hangout. My curiosity won out, and I followed him without saying a word. We made our way among the all-male crowd to a narrow stairway going down to the basement. He opened the door at the foot of the stairs, and we walked into what appeared to be La Traviata's dressing room, filled with feathers, wigs, dresses and photographs of herself, and famous movie actresses: Garbo and Maria Felix were the overwhelming favorites. She had taken off her wig, but was still wearing her red dress. As we entered, she was taking off her pendant earrings.

"You were wonderful tonight," Marcos said to her.

"Thank you, thank you. Please, sit down," she said smiling, while removing her wig and feathers from the only two chairs in the room.

"This is our man," the old man continued; I sensed a certain sexual connotation in his voice, but I was wrong, he was all business. "This is Angel Romero," he said, introducing me to the star.

"Sit down, please," Angel said. "Well, Marcos must have told you about our plans to integrate the community in exile, especially the artists and intellectuals. It's been very difficult for us to find someone who would be acceptable to us as well as the exiles. It seems that you're it."

"Wait a minute."

"Just let me finish, okay?"

I felt ridiculous talking politics to a man wearing a shinny red dress, removing mascara from his left eye.

"Listen, Miguel—can I call you Miguel?" I didn't react, so he continued, looking at me through the mirror, "Cuba cannot continue the way it is now; you can be part of the process that will change things. What we want is for you to go to Havana for the January celebration of the Revolution's twentieth birthday as a guest of the government, and read one of your poems as a gesture of goodwill between the exile community and the Cubans in the island; you can be instrumental in uniting our people. You will be free to go anywhere, to do anything, to talk to anyone."

"I'm sorry," I said, cutting him short, "you have the wrong man."

"You don't have to answer now," he said, turning to me, with his face full of cold cream. "Think it over; Marcos will get in touch with you with the details. Don't say anything else now. Please, just think it over."

I went up the narrow staircase, past the ad-mixture of male hookers, seductive looks, and anxious eyes and out onto the street. With pimps, prostitutes, drunks and potential muggers, I went up Eighth Avenue.

Again and again I repeated in my mind the conversation with

the two unorthodox revolutionaries at the gay club in an attempt to recapture every gesture, every word; in an attempt to find some catch in their motives; in an attempt to decipher them and test myself.

Marcos was right in his evaluation of our situation. I didn't think their revolutionary means justified the end, but at the same time I wasn't walking hand-in-hand with the exile groups. I couldn't agree with their refusal to get rid of their past, nor with their political narrowmindedness.

The exiles admired my work, but distrusted me. Now it happened that those in Cuba also admired me, but I distrusted them. They were clearly wanting to use me, but I didn't know for what. I couldn't be vain enough to think that they really needed me. Governments don't need poets.

I felt I was caught in the middle of something. Either side could let me have it at any moment if I wasn't careful.

As I crossed 47th Street, I heard my name called out several times. It was Marcos. Out of breath, struggling to run he had come after me. I stopped and turned around. The old man arrived at 47th Street panting.

"Please, don't go. Just listen to me for a minute, please."

"All right. Let's go in here," I said pointing to a Greek coffee shop.

We sat in a booth and ordered two coffees. The old man, still out of breath, began talking.

"Listen, my son, you have to help me. I'm in deep trouble." He was breathing heavily. His eyes were those of a frightened man, of a desperate man. I didn't understand why.

"They had questioned me about you. I had promised that you were ready, that you were convinced."

"How come?"

"I had followed you, I had studied you. I am a good judge of character. I was certain you would say yes."

"Well, I'm sorry but ... "

"You can't say no," the old man interrupted with a cracked voice, He took out his handkerchief and wiped his forehead, then continued. "I'm in trouble. I'm sixty-seven years old. I'm a tired revolutionary. My wife died some years ago. My oldest son was killed during the Bay of Pigs Invasion. My grandson, Luisito, is of military age. I'm the only one who can help him. Because of me he has not been sent to fight in Angola. As a matter of fact, recruiting you was my latest endeavor to keep him from going into the army. If you don't come to Cuba, he goes to Africa."

"Damn it, why me?"

"I don't know. You seemed like a good prospect. You know, last year we had the Committee of 75 in Havana. Fidel put them all in his pocket. He actually challenged me, Fidel. He told me to bring to Cuba a member of the exile community who was neither in favor nor against the Revolution, preferably an artist or an intellectual. This person would then become the pivot around which a new, real dialogue could be established. The truth is, my son, that you are my last hope. At this point in my life I couldn't care less about the Revolution, or Fidel or Cuba. I just want to save my boy."

"I don't know," I said.

"Think about it, please."

"All right. I'll think about it."

3

I would not give my alarm clock the pleasure of sounding off at 8:30 a.m. with its usual burst of simplified and rebroadcasted news of mutilated children, fires at apartment dwellings in a ghetto or some atrocious murder in the subway. Good morning through WINS. I tried in vain to talk to Antonio all day long; by the time I got in touch with him, it was nearly seven in the evening, and he was going out to pick up a girlfriend. We agreed to meet at the Ansonia Hotel where he was rehearsing a play for an Off-Broadway theater. We both arrived at the lobby of the old building almost simultaneously—I by 73rd street and he by 74th.

As he walked towards me with fluid and brisk steps, puffing on an eternal cigarette, wearing suit and tie, dark glasses and a distracting smile as if on his way up the isle to receive an Oscar, he shouted, "Hi, brother I'm gonna introduce you to this American chick; you'll love her, she's an actress and is ready. You won't have to talk much to her; nothing like those Cuban girls, to whom you have to give those Shakespearean monologues before you take them to bed."

They might have been rehearsing at the studio on the second floor, but he was giving a performance all by himself as usual. I tried to tell him I needed to talk; I tried to impress him with the fact that l was in the middle of a conspiracy, which he dismissed with a careless "Don't worry about it, we'll talk after dinner, okay? We'll take these girls to your apartment, and then, you know."

I couldn't stand the guy; he would drop anything, no matter how important, when he was trying to make it with a new woman. "Damn it, Antonio, I have to talk to you," I shouted back.

"Listen, we're pals or what?" he said. "Let me make it with this girl, I've been after her for months, okay?" Once again sex won over politics. I put my dilemma aside and began to wonder what the other girl looked like; I just hoped if it came down to having to make it with her, that she wouldn't get romantic.

The rehearsal was over, and out came the two actresses. Antonio's girlfriend was a knockout, of course; the other one, however, was short and plump. Her outfit wasn't exactly out of Bloomingdale's; it was rather middle-America in the fifties. She was perspiring profusely. By the time we got into Antonio's white 1970 Cadillac, I felt nauseated. No one wanted to have dinner, so we headed for my place. One step in the door, and I had the record player going, in a desperate attempt to expedite matters. Antonio commenced with his *modus operandi*. I sat on the carpet, next to my date; we drank, the music played, hands touched, and I was forced to ask her to follow me into the bedroom. Oh, an ugly object hurts me like a wound ...

After the ordeal, I sat on the bed, leaning against the wall. Marcos, the old man, came to my mind; I heard Antonio talking in the living room; I figured he was through, so I went over. All four of us were naked; Antonio had just rolled a joint, which he passed to his girlfriend. My nameless date sat next to her actress friend on the couch; Antonio sat on a rocker; I went back to the floor. "You're ready now," I asked him with a sigh.

"Shoot," he answered, while removing some particles of Colombian leaf from the tip of his tongue.

"I was approached yesterday by the Cuban government."

"You're kidding?"

"No, I'm not kidding."

"What the hell do they want from you?"

"They want me to go to Cuba, to see for myself what is happening there, they want me to read a poem during the celebration of the anniversary of the Revolution; I guess they want me to open the door for others who are still undecided."

"Undecided about what? What the shit is this? They're screwing you up; they want to use you. Don't you see?"

"Yes, I see."

"What did you say? You're not going, of course."

"I don't know"

"What are you talking about? Are you crazy or something? You know how long it took me to convince everyone here that you're okay? You must be crazy; what the fuck is this. I stood up for you."

"That's just it, Antonio."

"What do you mean?"

"Why the hell do you have to convince anyone about me?"

"Don't be childish," he said with disappointment and disgust, as he walked to the kitchen. His dark, skinny and hairy body typified the revolutionary Casanova. He returned with a glass of wine and smoking a cigarette. In a more relaxed tone of voice, he seemed to be thinking out loud. "We have to try to put ourselves in their place. What are they after? That's what we have to find out. It they have come to this, it means that they're scared; they must be having lots of problems at home, and they want to show the people in Cuba that the exiles are really not against their government." He appeared satisfied with his own rationalization. He paused, took a drag off his cigarette, and then continued, "You know, this is the break we have been waiting for." With that one he really baffled me. He turned to the girls, who had endured our mystifying dialogue in Spanish, and asked them to get dressed; then he began to put on his clothes with a soliloquy about some plans, retaliation and what not. We said a hasty goodbye; they left, I closed the door—still naked—and caught a glance of myself in the mirror, visible through the open bathroom door.

The following morning, Antonio called. He said he was getting people together, that plans were being made. I didn't bother to ask about any of it, having decided the night before to discard the whole matter: Antonio, the old man, Cuba and the exiles.

THANKS, BUT ...

One afternoon in November I met Ariadne, the political activist beauty from Hunter College, walking along Lexington Avenue near 59th Street. She had been shopping; I was walking home, after spending the day at the Public Library. My desire to see her betrayed my ambiguous game to avoid her. With a circus of peddlers, shoppers, taxis, buses and pollution rushing by, we talked for a few moments; then she asked me if I would like to go to her house for Thanksgiving. Her father, who was a waiter, was going to be working; only her mother and her cousin would be there. They were having a Cuban Thanksgiving, she warned me; the turkey had given way to a roast pork loin, white rice, black bean soup and fried green plantains. How could I resist? Around seven-thirty, I got to her house. Dinner was ready, and being from the countryside they ate early. Without hesitation we went into the dining room. In the living room the television set was on; a Venezuelan soap opera was castigating the empty furniture.

The meal didn't last long. By the time we finished eating, the soap opera was still going on, or was it another one? With coffee, however, the conversation picked up. Somehow we got to talking about illnesses. Ariadne's mother began telling us about a time when one of her brothers had a stomach ache.

"Look, my boy, they took a glass like this," she said, taking an empty glass from the table to demonstrate as she went along, "and they put it upside-down on his belly, where he had the pain. When they took off the glass, his skin was red as anything, but the pain was gone. The thing is that people here are too advanced. Right away they want to go to the doctor."

"There are things that one cannot believe in, but there are others that one can believe in," the cousin said very philosophically. He had arrived two years before from Spain, where he had gone

101

when he left Cuba. The last eight or ten months he spent on the island, he had been working in the fields, like everyone else that applied for a visa to leave the country.

"When my sister Soledad was small," he continued, "she had a fever that lasted about ten days. She didn't eat. She was pale and skinny, and wide-eyed. And my father said, 'We have to take this girl to Havana.' We was all set to take Soledad to Havana, when a woman tells my mother, 'Listen, you should take your daughter to the spiritualist center that is close by.' At that point, my mother would have done anything; she was desperate. Well, we took my sister to that center. As we were entering, the *espiritista* said to my mother, 'Jesus, lady, your daughter has the evil eye. My God, she has a ball in her stomach. When she lets go of it, you won't believe it. Listen, you give her this water to drink. You'll see how she is going to get well.' Let me tell you, the next day Soledad began to vomit this green gook with a stench that was out of this world. My mother took such a fright; and then she said, 'Juanito'—he's my father—'we have to believe in something.' Since that day, Soledad hasn't even caught a cold. There are people who simply cheat, and make a living from that, but there are others who don't; they simply give you a little water to drink, and they cure you."

"In my house," the mother interrupted, "when one of the boys had either vomit of diarrhea, my mother went to the backyard, to the anon tree and she'd break off a little branch. If he was vomiting, she'd pull the branch upward; if it was diarrhea, then she'd pull it downward. Then she'd make a tea from it, and she'd make him drink it. Well, that was the end of the illness."

The cousin laughed wholeheartedly. He drank the last sip from his coffee, and continued, "You know what the men used to do in agriculture, working in the fields? The moment you filled the papers to leave the country, you lost everything you had, and they would send you to what they called *Agricultura*, working in the fields harvesting potatoes, or coffee, or cutting sugar cane, or simply picking up stones. Really. And that could last sometimes three or four years, or as long as they took to give you a visa to leave. Well, the men would take a clove of garlic and stick it up their ass, yeah. In no time they'd run up so high fever that you wouldn't believe it. Then he was rushed to the doctor who would right away send him home."

Still laughing he continued, "There were others who would swallow a piece of cotton. They would take him for X-Rays, and the cotton came out in the X-Rays. They would think he had ulcers so they'd send him home. You know, you could go into the country and you would ask a *guajiro*, 'Listen, I have this or that,' and he would get some herbs to cure you with. No one went to the doctor. Now everyone wants to go to the doctor. Faith can cure you. You can say, 'This is not going to happen to me,' and it doesn't happen."

The mother approached the table and sat down. "Let me tell you something. Sometimes one has to go to the doctor, but there are home remedies for everything. There are more than twenty thousand different herbs that can cure you. There was a man named Cardo, who was the overseer of a large farm. He was always screaming and cursing. He would drive his pick-up truck like a madman all over the countryside. One day his wife had a dream. She dreamed that her husband had had a car accident in which their daughter had died. An what do you think happened? The next day, Cardo went out in his truck, angry as always, cursing and yelling. He hit a big tree. The impact threw him to one side, while his daughter was thrown the other way. He was lying there, bleeding. An old man approached him and said, 'Don't move that man,' and he took him to a spiritualist center nearby, and he saved him."

"I believe in that," the cousin said. "If I only speak Spanish, for instance, and I am healing you, and you are American and only speak English, and a spirit of one of your English-speaking relatives enters me and I begin to speak English fluently, you have to believe. There are many things in life, you know. Haven't you entered a house sometime and felt a strong vapor behind your ears, as if it was pulling you back? It is that there is some evil there, someone who wants to do you harm. It has happened to me."

"Have you ever been to a Chinese funeral?" the mother asked, her eyes sparkling with delight "Well, they put cans of sardines and things like that in the coffin of the dead Chinese, so that when he gets up there he's prepared in case he gets hungry. Or what happened to Carmen's daughter," she continued without breaking her line of thought. "She died of an illness that no one ever knew what it was. Carmen was unconsolable. She had lost all desire to live, so they took her to a spiritualist center. It was about two months since her daughter had died. The *espiritista* told her to go to the cemetery at midnight and open her daughter's grave. They were to give the corpse two small blows on the back, and she would wake-up, because the girl wasn't dead. She had had an attack of something or other. Then they had to take two blouses and a dress and leave them by the grave. They did all that, and then they left. Sometime later, a man who lived by the cemetery noticed the foul smell and went over to investigate; he found the open grave and the decomposed body. To make a long story short, Carmen and her husband got ten years in jail each. The *espiritista* was never caught, I think she moved to another town. After that incident, the people in town said that the girl had not come home as the spiritualist had expected because they hadn't left her any money for the bus."

On that note, everyone got up and moved to the living room; another soap opera was about to start. I also got up slowly, and said good night; Ariadne walked me to the door; I kissed her and left. It was a cold night. I decided to walk, head east on 23rd Street, and north on First Avenue. Potholes, like moon craters on the chronically deteriorating Manhattan streets, couldn't conceal their battered faces beneath the glare of traffic lights that progressed like electronic soldiers from green to yellow to a determinate red, only to repeat the exercise as a nostalgic mania. It was a night beset by tidbits of sadness, with no glee, no allure; a night to harvest perceptions, its persistent emptiness evoking an epiphany.

On my way home, I passed by the Havana East Restaurant on 73rd. Street, and decided to walk in. Carlos Valle was playing the piano, singing, and smiling, making fingers dance on table-tops, making bodies sway frantically under veil of perspiration, the bartender performing his well rehearsed acrobatics with the piña colada. Lawyers, dentists, office workers, nurses, secretaries and car salesmen drank their rum and coke and forgot their sorrows, their relatives in Cuba, their unpaid bills: bottled escape shared between songs and mystified nostalgia. Meanwhile, the American clientele sat in the back room eating their black bean soup and rice. Centerstage, however, the natives were being faithful to their myths. Through the rampant abandon of hips, thighs and cha-cha, I made my way until I could no longer move; breasts, shoulders, flowing hair and smiles held me in place. A woman danced in front of me; I didn't know her, but she pretended we were together. I grabbed her behind; still smiling, she said, "Wait, don't make a mistake." To which I answered with a bouncing smile, "Why, is that not your ass?" Entering the restaurant was like traveling two thousand miles, like breaking the time barrier, the twilight zone: a living science fiction movie. As if sleepwalking, I had arrived in Cuba, the Havana East had transformed itself into the Tropicana Night Club of pre- Castro days.

Oldtimers were there to relive their (perhaps fictional) past, and at the same time alleviate their feeling of displacement; music, laughter and rum were the catharsis. From a *guaracha*, Carlos turned to a *ranchera*, a typical Mexican song. Nothing short of being a pseudo-masochist would help anyone sing a good *ranchera*: in it, the most pathetic suffering described in the most pathetic way conceivable would mingle with desperate cries—Ayayayaya-yayayayay—echoes of a broken heart or a lost soul. *Rancheras* are a poor man's emotional release, it takes the place of an analyst. An overweight woman, with oversized eyeglasses played a tambourine out of tempo and too loud. Everyone clapped their hands and sang along, while at the bar there was a battle to the death between daiquiris and scotch and sodas. Carlos continued to exhort them to dance, to sing, to forget—in that order—as in an esoteric spiritual encounter; his laughter shined brighter than the crescendos of his piano.

The night sneered at the passage of time, shrugged its alcoholic shoulders past 3 a.m., and watched the exhausted dancers file out slowly, half drunk, but high with spirits which would last them the whole week, or at least the weekend. Around four o'clock, a middle-aged couple came in; there were few of us left in the place, either diehards or faithful friends, who had decided to make it to the end. The newcomer was wearing a curly toupee that made him look like a Cuban Shirley Temple in drag. With an aging boxer's wave of the hand he greeted those at the bar, and continued to the men's room. The woman, in a luminously intoxicating pink dress, a wooden hairdo and violet lipstick that drew her receding lips into an involuntary grimace, sat next to me; she took out her compact, surveyed with suspicion how the fourth rendition of her night's makeup was surviving. "I can't stand it," she said, putting away her compact. She then gestured to the bartender for what seemed to be her usual drink. "I have lots of kidney problems," she said, turning to me. With a Betty Davis gesture, she lit a cigarette, said hello to Carlos still at the piano and went on, "Can you imagine, they just gave me six months to live?" I didn't answer and she couldn't care less, for she was not addressing me, I was simply her excuse to ramble on. By then, her husband was out of the men's room, and was sitting at a table in the next room, talking to the owner. Then she continued, "I wasn't feeling all together well; you know, I was sort of sad and depressed, I don't know. I called a friend of mine and told her about it, and she told me to go over right away, that in the Bronx there was a woman that was terrific. What do you mean terrific, I said, I'm dying in six months, I mean, it didn't make sense. I didn't want a female lover, but then she told me that the woman was one of those who communicates with saints, with spirits, with African gods and I don't know what else;

well, I never believed in African saints, I'm sorry but it's the truth; Christ, the Virgin Mary and St. Christopher I could understand, but what did I have to do with an African god. Anyway I live in Union City, in New Jersey, you know, so it isn't so easy for me to go to the Bronx; I don't drive, and if I tell my husband to take me to the Bronx to see an African god I think he would divorce me right there, not that it would be a great loss, but anyway I told my friend yes, and she said she would pick me up. I didn't know what else to do, doctors couldn't save me or anything so I told her to come and pick me up. Can I tell you, we walked into that woman's house in the Bronx, and I had not finished saying hello when she said to me, 'You have six months to live,' which I knew already, but how did she know?"

Carlos had finished his set by then, and he came over and sat with us. "What were you saying about six months?" he asked her.

"A woman in the Bronx told me that I had six months to live. Well, a doctor had told me that already, but she confirmed it, and she didn't know me. She was the one who told me my kidneys were in terrible shape. I had had an ulcer some time ago, but I was cured by then." With the thumb and middle fingers of her right hand she pressed against her temples. "Everything is in the mind," she continued.

"Everything," Carlos said.

"And nerves."

"Listen," I said. "How can you pay attention to people like that?"

"How much did she charge you?" Carlos asked.

"Fifty."

"Do you believe that?"

"That's a racket they have."

"She would ask me, 'You want to ask me something? Go ahead and ask.' No, no, I don't want to ask you anything, I said, I want you to tell me. So she told me, 'I don' t give you more than six months.' That's why I don't care anymore. I just want to have a good time from now on. You know , the next day I went to work, and I looked horrible. Everyone was asking me what was wrong. When I told them that I had six months to live, they all started laughing, saying, 'Don't be silly.' Well, you know, I also have stomach problems. You know, digestion. The food that takes a normal person two or three hours to digest, I digest in half an hour. Can you imagine? And then, since it gets to the intestines so fast, out it goes with the same speed, from either end."

I took that as my cue to leave; it was almost closing time anyhow. I said my goodbye's and slipped out the glass doors into the damp morning din. The nervous headlights from stumbling taxi-cabs made the soft drizzle more palpable, while the hungry roar of their tired engines sounded like an arduous buzz of bees after a tropical rainstorm. It had been a night for giving thanks; so it was.

2

After that Thanksgiving, I began to see more and more of Ari-adne, and through her, I again fell into the Cubaness that I had been trying to suppress for some time. Antonio had been out of town, he was organizing a march from Boston to Miami to dramatize—for the benefit of network television—Cuba's unending plight. As soon as he got back to New York, he organized a dinner party; four couples except for Cyndie, his girlfriend, were all Cuban. We gathered for dinner, but not exactly to eat. It took place on a Sat-urday night; it had been set for eight, but by nine-thirty we had all arrived. As if by design, each couple brought a bottle of Spanish wine, a loaf of Cuban bread and some sort of dessert. Ariadne and I arrived first. Cyndie had spent all day at Antonio's, and had done the cooking. Manolo Cueto and his wife, Daisy, arrived next. Manolo was an ex-political prisoner from Castro's jail at Bo-niato, in Oriente; he was a man of deep convictions, few words, an exuberant laughter and a volcanic belly. His wife was sort of attractive, with warm, bright red hair—not common for women from the island—who was a tease; a woman of simple tastes, from whose mouth emanated a deluge of words. She must have been a good sexual partner (she was actually another of my fantasies), but I never found out. The last to arrive were Rodolfo and his girlfriend, Linda.

After filling two hours with unintelligent conversation, and killing two bottles of wine from Spain, *Concha y Toro*, dinner was finally served. The menu consisted of a Cuban-Italian concoction with hints of Puerto Rican seasoning, made palatable by our deeply felt hunger and our love for the Newyorrican chef: "Give us this day our sexual fantasies, and we will eat anything she cooks."

"Do you know what the people in Cuba would give to have a dinner like this?" Manolo asked rhetorically.

"Don't ruin my dinner, please," Rodolfo said, "If you start to think about the people that are going hungry in Cuba, I won't be able to eat."

"People are going hungry all over," I said, "you don't have to go to Cuba to find them; right here in the Bronx, or in lower Man-hattan you'll find hundreds of them. Hunger is not a monopoly of communism; as a matter of fact, more people go hungry in the Dominican Republic or in any Central American country than in communist Cuba."

"I don't know," Cyndie said, "but from what I hear no one was exiled from Cuba because he was going hungry; as a matter of fact, most of the exiles weren't even persecuted."

"Where did you hear that?" Antonio asked. "From your communist teachers at Columbia University?"

"I thought that was common knowledge," she said.

"Common ignorance," Antonio said.

"The problem is that people in this country don't know anything," Manolo said, "Americans don't know and they don't care. All they want is their McDonalds, their football games and their two week-vacation in the summer."

"We have a different view of things," I said, "because we have been forced out of our country ." Rodolfo's girlfriend, a Cuban born model raised in France, smiled at all that was going on. Knowing Rodolfo, he must have given her a pass of cocaine before coming to dinner, in order to disassociate her from our political tete-a-tete. Except for hello, she did not utter a word all night; by the time she left she was too drunk to even say goodnight.

"Daisy wanted to go to Italy next summer," Manolo said, "but after all the spaghetti I was forced to eat in prison, I can't stand being in a country where they eat spaghetti every day."

"That's probably all they could get from Russia," Antonio said.

"Where did you hear that they had spaghetti in Russia?" Cyndie asked.

"Remember that time we went to Little Italy?" Rodolfo asked me, "When you started a fight?"

"What happened?" Manolo's wife asked.

"We were at Puglia's," Rodolfo said, "eating and carrying on with the fat woman that sings there; we sang old Cubans songs, and old Mexican songs, and old songs from everywhere. At the table behind Miguel there were two couples, and one of the guys was telling the others about a time when he used to work for the C.I.A. in Miami, and he used to send Cuban exiles into phony commando raids inside Cuba. Well, after about ten minutes of that, Miguel couldn't take it any longer; he picked up the tray of steaming clams with red sauce that had just been brought to our table, got up, turned around and poured it on the guy's head. Shit, that man shot up like a devil; he wanted to kill Miguel, but the little waiter with the toupee that always took care of us grabbed the guy from behind while Miguel began to insult him, 'You fucking,

son-of-a-bitch, damned American Imperialist ... ' He was ready to
punch the guy, so I grabbed him from behind and forced him out
of the restaurant; the waiter was still holding the American. Since
we hadn't eaten, we continued down to Chinatown. I don't think
we ever went back to Little Italy."

"Since when are you a fighter?" Ariadne asked me.

"I'm not," I said, "the guy just pissed me off."

"That's enough of that," Rodolfo said, "let's forget Cuba. I just
want to ask the women something, let me drink some wine first ...
I want to know who likes anal sex."

"What?" everyone asked in unison. Laughter broke out, nervous laugher, guilty laughter.

"Let's be honest now," Rodolfo said.

"Don't ask me," one of the girls said; "That must be painful,"
another one said.

Rodolfo got up, with a glass in his left hand and laughing his
head off said, "I love it. To me all openings are good."

"You're a pig," Cyndie said.

"Have you tried it?" Manolo asked her. She brushed off the
question with an intense glance, followed by a smile. At that point
we knew that to stop any political discussion all one had to do was
to bring up anal sex. The women began to clear the table, and
from the kitchen we could hear the giggling; were they comparing
notes? We ended the discussion with ambiguous anecdotes (no
names, of course). After the coffee, I decided to play a theater
game in which we would improvise a scene about a Cuban family:
the confrontation between an old, right-wing father and his son.
The action was to take place in Miami, in the seventies. I asked
Antonio to play the father, since the character suited his personality
perfectly, and Ariadne to play his wife; I played the part of the son.
We rearranged some of the furniture in Antonio's dining room;
he sat at the table, Ariadne went to the kitchen, and I came in.
Antonio (the father) was talking to himself.

FATHER (Antonio): They're pushing me too far.

MOTHER (Ariadne): What's the matter, honey?

FATHER: Same old thing.

SON: Send everyone to hell.

FATHER: Yeah, everyone to hell? You can't be so radical.

SON: Then, stop complaining.

MOTHER: Well, what is it?

SON: Don't ask him now, he's really steaming

FATHER: Don't be funny.

MOTHER: Please, don't start again; I have a splitting headache.

FATHER: It's easy for him to be a liberal, he doesn't have to go
   out and break his back to make a living.

SON: What do you want me to do? Become a used car salesman,
   like you?

MOTHER: It's not like being president of the country, but it's not
   the end of the world either.

SON: He probably would have wanted me to be a redneck like
   him, to be a policeman, to go into the army. That's our
   family's profession: beating up innocent people.

FATHER: You can do with your life whatever you want, and I
   never beat up anyone, you hear?

SON: How about those stories you used to tell about the good old
   days.

FATHER: Don't confuse law and order with beating up innocent
   people.

MOTHER: I can't stand this any longer; both of you are going to
   drive me crazy.

FATHER: It's your fault, you made him that way.

SON: Must you always blame everyone else for everything?

FATHER: (*Rushing towards his son*) Let me tell you something.

MOTHER: My, God, this is all I needed. Stop it.

SON: Go on, hit me; you're good at that.

FATHER: You're asking for it.

MOTHER: This is what we have come to? What a sight! We have
   come so far, we have gone through so much, I think it
   would have been better ... (*to her son*) You were right,
   your father spends his time selling used cars, making revolution, smoking cigars, and you go to college, or out with
   your friends, and I stay here, inside these four walls, like
   a prisoner. Well, I'll tell you both something, I can't stand
   it any more. I'm tired, you hear me? One of these days
   I'll pack my bags, and you'll never see me again.

FATHER: Where are you going to go, to Cuba?

MOTHER: Anywhere. I didn't come to this country to rot.

FATHER: I don't know what all of you want from me? I cannot
   change, I cannot forget, I cannot stop feeling.

MOTHER: Nobody wants you to change, honey, nobody wants you
   to leave anything; we have already left enough behind. It
   isn't that.

SON: It isn't that, dad, it's ... it's my fault.

FATHER: No, it's not your fault, or anyone else's fault. The problem is that we're here, and not in our country, the problem
   is that we're no longer what we were.

MOTHER: We know that, but we have to go on, we can't continue
to live looking back. We eat, we have color television, we
have a car, so what?

FATHER: If I get up tomorrow, and forget all about that little,
shitty island where I was born, where I grew up, where I
still have relatives, where many of my friends either died
or are still in jail, what the hell am I?

SON: The question is not to forget, dad. Take me or my friends;
you have a life to remember, but in that life we are nothing, we don't belong, because we have nothing to share
with you in that life. We don't belong there, and we don't
belong here; we just don't belong. We're not Cubans and
we're not Americans.

FATHER: You are Cuban all right. You're young, your life is ahead
of you; our lives, your mother's and mine, are behind; we
don't even dance the *rumba* any more. Do you want to
know if you're Cuban, wait until you hear a good *rumba*;
if you're Cuban you won't be able to stand still.

"Fuck it, Antonio. Do you always have to end everything with
music?" I had to exclaim—out of character—and that was the end
of our little melodrama.

"That wasn't bad," Ariadne said, "it sounded as if we had mem-
orized the lines."

"Those are lines any Cuban would have said," Antonio exclaimed, "but let me try another little play."

Rolando interrupted, "Before this theater-in-exile continues, let
me open another bottle of wine." During the intermission, some
went to the bathroom, some commented on our play, some joked at
our expense and Manolo and his wife excused themselves saying
that it was too late, and left. Once we were back in the dining
room, Antonio prepared the scene he wanted to improvise.

"We are in Cuba; it's April of 1961. The Bay of Pigs Invasion
has ended in a fiasco. We are in the theater of the Cuban Workers
Federation. I am a prisoner, and Miguel, you are a journalist who
is questioning me, okay?"

I agreed, and we began.

JOURNALIST: Good evening, ladies and gentlemen, Mr. President, foreign ambassadors, members of the government,
and all of our television viewers. Comrades, today, April
24th, 1961, as it has been said, we have organized this
encounter in order to give a group of journalists the opportunity to question, in your presence, some of the prisoners captured by our rebel army, and our revolutionary

militia some days ago at Playa Giron. In the name of the
government, I must ask you to please remain silent. (*To
the prisoner*) What is you name?

PRISONER: Roberto Fuentes

JOURNALIST: To what unit did you belong?

PRISONER: To the second Battalion, Company "G."

JOURNALIST: Will you answer every question that we ask you?

PRISONER: Those that are in my power, yes.

JOURNALIST: Where were you trained?

PRISONER: In the mountains of Guatemala.

JOURNALIST: How long were you there?

PRISONER: About twenty days.

JOURNALIST: Why did you leave Cuba?

PRISONER: For personal reasons. I had a certain economic position ... I was forced to leave the country in 1959.

JOURNALIST: If you weren't in politics, why did you feel the
Revolution was against you, making you join the invasion?

PRISONER: Well, these two years since the triumph of the Revolution I've been out of the country. Everyone said Cuba
was communist; I am not a communist, I am a nationalist. I thought that we had left an imperialist country to
join another. I felt a sense of obligation.

JOURNALIST: Are you a nationalist in the way that Batista was
a nationalist?

At that point Rodolfo interrupted, "I've heard this bullshit before."

Ariadne asked him to be quiet, but it was Antonio who responded to his outburst, "The trouble with you," he began, "is
that you couldn't care less about Cuba."

To which Rodolfo answered, "And the trouble with you, Antonio, is that you're full of shit. You're all fucking crazy. Why don't
you stop it with that old song and dance. Let's talk of something
else; Nicaragua, the weather, anything."

Antonio, getting more and more excited with each word, answered, "We all have our hang-ups; you like cocaine and orgies,
we talk about Cuba."

Rodolfo, cracking a smile said, "Yeah, but at least I do something with my hang-up, all you do is talk. I don't see any of you
taking a rifle and going there to fight; you're all nightclub revolutionaries."

Antonio had just about all he could stand. He rushed towards
Rodolfo, hitting the dining table so hard that he broke his glass.

Between the screaming, the broken glass, the cursing and the cries of the women, hell broke loose. Slowly, we all settled down and began cleaning up the mess. Rodolfo, our harshest critic,was the most handsomest of the group; he was also the most outspoken, opinionated and dogmatic. He was a salesman and part-time actor, tall and tanned, always up-to-date on the latest Italian fashions. His gestures were slow and precise, as if measured, as if economizing every possible movement. He was a man of interminable monologues, occasionally had tinged with loneliness which he alleviated by talking his head off. We all decided to call it a night.

Around ten the following morning, the phone rang. It was Antonio who insisted in seeing me right away. In the weeks since I had told him about my encounter with the old man Marcos, he had been having meetings with his colleagues; they had taken my invitation to visit Cuba quite seriously, and were planning "something big;" it was dangerous to talk over the phone. I was asleep when the phone rang, and Antonio's conversation sounded like a dream. Yawning, I asked him to come over, while I took a shower and got dressed; by then I would be in a more agreeable mood to listen to what sounded like a far-fetched scheme. The reason for the dinner the night before was that he wanted to talk to me then, and since we hadn't spoken for a while he didn't know how to approach me. As it turned out, the dinner was a fiasco and his plan went out the window. Less than forty minutes later, he arrived; I was making coffee, wearing a towel around my waist. Antonio sat on a rocker, and I came over with a pot and two cups; after removing some books and papers from the couch, I sat facing him. He asked me to turn on the television, so that we would not be heard. He put three teaspoons of sugar in his coffee and lit a cigarette.

"You know," Antonio began, "since I saw you last I haven't stopped. I've been everywhere. I have met with some important people here and in Miami concerning your visit. Plans are being made. They know who that guy Marcos is. It is true that he works for the Cuban government. As a matter of fact, he is a high government official. We have checked-up on him. We haven't been able to determine what the hell they're planning, but it definitely is something big. Why they contacted you in particular, we don't know."

Antonio moved incessantly as he spoke, gesticulating, smoking one cigarette after another, taking off and putting on his sun glasses, which he wore even at night, crossing and uncrossing his legs, leaning forward and sitting on the edge of his seat, and going back and taking a long drag from his cigarette.

"We don't know what they're up to. We have some idea, but we're not sure," Antonio said. "Through certain clandestine means we're trying to find out though. Meanwhile, we have a plan of our own. We are going to take advantage of the situation. This is a very propitious moment for action. You know as well as I do that it's almost impossible for us to prepare an invasion from this country, the Americans have our hands tied. We cannot get funds, arms, people. Our men are under surveillance. You, however, are not. No one suspects you." By then I had drank two cups of coffee, listening intensely, in total amazement. "You are not directly involved with any anti-Castro groups," Antonio continued. "That, I think is the crux of the matter. You are a poet, an intellectual, you are recognized as an important figure by everyone, yet you are not aligned with either side. You are the perfect man. We plan an act of aggression inside Cuba. We cannot do anything from the outside, therefore we have to make things happen inside. The people are ready to revolt. We know that for a fact, all they need is a push, an open act of violence, and they will follow. I am telling you, the time is ripe, it cannot fail, we are making sure of that."

I understood where Antonio was leading to. The leaders of the anti-Castro movements had chosen me to play hero for them. They wanted to put me on the mythical white horse, on which men like them had put José Martí a hundred years before, on his way to his death. As they had done to him, they wanted to make a martyr out of me. But I was going to have no part of it.

"Fuck it, Antonio," I said.

"Brother, we need you. The country needs you," he said, with an honesty that began to hurt.

"Don't give me that bull," I said.

"Miguel, believe me, you're the only one who can do this. Imagine the position you're in. You're going to come face to face with Fidel. Do you know how many people would give their lives for a chance like that?"

"Forget it, Antonio," I said.

"*Coño*, brother, don't fail me. I've been saying all sorts of good things about you."

"Don't defend me."

"All right, I won't defend you."

We were screaming at each other from the tops of our lungs.

"Great, just forget it," I said.

"I won't forget it," he insisted.

"Fuck it, Antonio, I don't want to talk about it. Can you understand that? What the hell are you trying to do? I am not going to commit suicide. I went through that already. I am not a gunman, I am not a soldier, I am not a martyr. Besides, I've decided not to go. I want nothing to do with any of this. I am not going to be a patsy for you or for them, or for anyone. This is your war, Antonio. Fight it by yourself."

We both remained silent, each looking away from the other. Antonio sighed, lit a cigarette and began speaking, measuring each word.

"Miguel, brother, I met you a few months ago, but we are very close nonetheless. I have come to love you as a good friend, and I think you feel the same way. I am not stupid, I may be fooling around, fucking around all the time. However, when it comes to Cuba, I'm dead serious. You know that. I wouldn't have asked you to do this if someone else could do it. I wouldn't ask you to give your life if I weren't willing to give mine. I would kill that son-of-a-bitch right now if I could, even if it cost me my life; I don't give a shit for my life. I am vegetating here; I spend days just thinking what the hell I can do for my country, and then I realize there's nothing I can do. I hit my head against the walls."

There was a long pause, then he continued, "Fidel is the only thing that stands in the way to a solution for our country. He sold out the Revolution. He ruined the country; he has been the cause of the death of thousands, of the hatred among brothers. We have to kill him, Miguel."

His voice began to crack. Antonio looked out the window. He had a lump in his throat. His face became almost distorted. It was a beautiful morning in New York. How many mornings like this one had seen Cuban exiles ploting against the government of the island, and planing invasions since the 1850's? From the frantic doings of Narciso Lopez—who wasn't even Cuban. He was born in Venezuela—with all his abortive plans to invade the island, to the poet Heredia, and the philosopher Saco and Father Varela, to José Martí and the thousands of men and women who lived in this city while their minds were among the palm trees a thousand miles away. So many Cuban tears had been shed inside simple rooms like this, so many arguments, fights and hopes.

On television a young, pregnant blond woman had just won $10,000 in "MATCH GAME." Antonio and I were silent and motionless. After a long pause, Antonio got up, approached me, and tapped me on the knee.

"I have to go, brother. I'll see you later," he said softly.

He walked out without saying anything else. I had remained motionless staring out the window, not seeing anything: I was looking inward. The sun was bright as it always is in the Caribbean, where nothing hides from it, where everything is defined by it and influenced by it. I imagined Martí must have been in a spot like the one I found himself in. But Martí knew what he wanted, and what he was doing. Martí did have a mission. It must have been on a sunny day like this that he wrote:

> Do not place me in shadows
> To die a traitor's death.
> I am good, and as such
> I will die facing the sun.

I could do nothing but wander about the apartment from room to room, finally stopping in the bathroom. I looked at myself in the mirror searching, but unable to think. Five minutes later I walked out and began walking towards Central Park. Crossing Madison Avenue against the light, I almost got hit by a taxi. The driver cursed at me in broken English.

I began to think back, to the time when Senator Mc Govern returned from Havana with a collegiate basketball team from South Dakota to spread Castro's gospel of baseball, preached against the sixteen-year-old American trade embargo against Cuba and the 1973 anti-hijacking agreement between the two countries. Mc Govern's tete a tete with Castro marked the final downfall of the Cuban exile movement as such.

Everyone of my compatriots who left the island in 1959 or soon after, did so with the conviction that he would return. Not in the distant future, but "In a few days." Later it became, "In a few months," until the eventual cry, "This Christmas Eve we'll be in Cuba." Nineteen Christmas Eves later, that notion had died. The Cuban exiles had accepted their fate, even though some hardline Cubans still had some idea of overthrowing Castro. For the majority, it was a thing of the past.

Since the birth of the Cuban Republic in 1902, the people of this island have had a very close relationship with the United States. Mainly because of the inability of Cubans to form lasting and honest governments. In the fifty-six year history of the Republic, there was a complete inability on the part of the Cubans to solve their own problems. Corrupt politicians plagued the country. The opposition in each case, trying to find a solution to the country's ailments, turned to the United States. This became the fastest way out. The Americans, on the other hand, since Cuba had an extremely valuable geographical position, always wanted the stability of the island.

The exiles, naively, were blindly led into the Bay of Pigs invasion because it was being prepared by *los americanos*. The Cubans asked no questions. If the Americans were behind it, they would follow. The Americans would help them fight communism, that's all they wanted to hear.

After the fiasco of the invasion, all the dozen or so anti-Castro movements continued their subversive activities, or at least in the majority of the cases they continued their discussions of their subversive activities. By then, it had become a way of life.

For most of the exiles, however, life had become a continuation of pre-Castro Cuba. They had to live in the past simply not to perish. They couldn't let go of their nostalgia. The fact was that these people had not been able to stop Castro. They had not been able to fight communism successfully, and they had not been able to sustain American's allegiance to their causes. They had been defeated physically at the Bay of Pigs invasion, emotionally by being forced to live from memories, and morally by Castro's ability to keep a hold on the country for almost twenty years. The release of some political prisoners, the easing of tension, and the possible reunification of some families had brought about, without question, the demise of the exiles as a political group.

And then, by some turn of fate, I had it in my powers to do what no other Cuban, the CIA, or the Mafia could do: assassinate Castro. Could I? Would I?

DO UT DEUS

"What do you think of all this?"

"I don't know."

"What do you mean, you don't know?"

"Well, it isn't my story."

"Not your story? You're writing it, aren't you?"

"I'm the writer all right, but you're the protagonist. It's your story."

"But you're writing it."

"I write it, but I have nothing to do with it."

"You don't really believe that."

"I'm only a writer."

"So am I."

"I'm not a revolutionary."

"Neither am I."

"All these things are beyond me."

"I am not part of that environment."

"Neither am I."

"..."

"I get the impression you and I could be one and the same."

"How would I know?"

THE SNAKE'S BITE

Early morning the following Tuesday, the brisk air of December was the only witness: a tall gray-haired man wearing a tan raincoat rang the bell of Antonio's apartment. It was an old, badly kept building on West 96th Street. Three Puerto Rican teenagers were throwing a football in the desolate street. Any hour of the day or night, one could find some Puerto Rican teenagers playing in the street, ducking cars, poking fun at the passersby. They would do anything to get out of the house, if their living quarters could be called a house. They were more like cages cramped with roaches, rats, filth and misery. It is tough growing up in the streets of New York, but it is worse having to grow up inside the tenements. An old man dragged himself up the street. A woman walked a dog. Behind a fourth-floor window, an old woman lethargically stared at the street below, not looking at anything in particular, simply letting her half-cataractal eyes travel over the garbage that covered the street and sidewalk. Newspapers and beer cans lay about like strange creatures. The new day promised nothing new for any of those people. It was one more day to survive, that was all.

When the doorbell rang, Antonio was reading the newspaper. He was wearing a dark blue bathrobe with red stripes. A record by Beny More was playing on the record player.

As he read, Antonio played with his moustache. The moustache gave his bony face a maturity that his thirty-one years hid quite well. It also made him look dark and full, a *Chulo*, a Cuban pimp. He was the cliche of a Caribbean latin lover. He walked the streets of New York as if he were walking in Havana. At every corner, someone said hello to him, invited him to a cup of espresso, or asked him for a loan. His political discourses were commonplace. Butchers, grocery store employees, waiters, they all treated him like a relative. Sitting in his living room that morning, Antonio looked

119

more like a well-to-do 19th Century French baron than a Cuban journalist reading his own editorial in the Sunday paper. He was the type of man that teenage girls find attractive but dangerous. But deep down he was a very dedicated man. Dedicated to his craft, to his compatriots, to the liberty of his homeland. Was it guilt? I asked myself. Conviction? Friendship? I don't know, but I hadn't been able to sleep for two days. I had decided to talk to Antonio; I needed to talk to him. It was past ten when I got to his house; I knew he usually slept late, I was sure to find him home. As I got to the lobby of the apartment building, a teenage boy was going out, so I let myself in without having to ring the bell. I took the stairs to the second floor, knocked at the door a couple of times, but he didn't answer; I noticed then that the door was unlocked. I pushed it softly and called out loud, "Is coffee ready?" I hesitated to go in, fearing he might be in there with a woman. I called out again, "Antonio, you're up?" No answer. I walked in, and in the middle of the living room, lying in a pool of blood, his face on top of the editorial he had just read a few minutes before, was Antonio's body, shot twice in the chest. His face still had that childish amazement that irritated me so much. I rushed to him, picked him up, turned him over in my arms and embraced him as I had embraced Mario Mar in Miami.

I embraced him and I cried as I had done the night Mario Mar died.

I embraced him and I shouted and I cursed, and all the emptiness of my life ran down my cheeks with his blood. Coming back from the supermarket, the woman next door had heard my cries and came in; the bag of groceries fell from her arms as she asked, "My boy, what are you doing?"

I looked at her, still holding Antonio's body in my arms, "He's dead, he's dead."

She called out, and a few moments later a man came in; I kept on repeating, "He's dead, he's dead."

The man grabbed me by the arms and tried to pull me away. "Come on, boy, come on, let him go, come on, let him go it's all right, come on." The woman took Antonio's body as it slid off my arms. The man went over to the phone and called the police; I wandered out the door, down the stairs and into the street. I walked and walked. Some forty or sixty blocks later, I stumbled into a Spanish grocery store somewhere in Washington Heights. A mulatto woman approached me as soon as I entered; my clothes were all stained with Antonio's blood. I was in a daze.

"My boy," she said, "there's an evil spirit in you; you need help." I didn't respond, she took my hand and pulled me out of the store, "Come with me," she said. Half a block away we entered an apartment building and walked down to the basement; it was pitch dark. She let go of my hand, took out a key, and opened a blue wooden door. The room was cold and damp. The only light in the basement came from a group of candles in front of an altar in one corner of the room. As my eyes got used to the darkness, I noticed there were lots of people in the room, some standing, others sitting; at another corner, three black men sat, each one of them had a drum in his arms. A woman who seemed to be in charge of whatever was going on, motioned to the three men in the corner, and they began playing. The three drums, each of a different tonality, established a counterpoint, as if holding a conversation, or a question-and-answer session. To the sound of the drums, the men began singing in what I thought was an African dialect; the people at the other end of the room also began chanting and clapping their hands, and then they began to sway, to shuffle their feet. The woman in charge wearing a red dress and an array of small bead necklaces around her neck, stood in front of the group with the altar to her back. The mulatto woman who had brought me to the religious basement where the ceremony was being held, went over to the altar and stretched out face down in front of it, with her arms stretched along her side; she got up, crossed her arms in front of her chest, and embraced the woman in red. She introduced me, and asked me to postrate myself as she had done. The woman in red touched me on the shoulders and muttered something unintelligible to me; she then grabbed me by the arms and brought me to my feet, crossed my arms over my chest and then embraced me. We moved to one side of the group. The incessant drums and chanting, all of a sudden changed rhythm, the tempo increased, and the chanting became louder. I felt as if I was loosing my balance. I felt my body move, the music became more intense; I was dancing, almost floating on air, my body was shaking, my eyes moved in all directions. The room began to go round and round; the beating of the drums and the chanting was almost unbearable; I couldn't see the faces of any of the people around me, seeing only colored lights flashing in front of my eyes. I felt water running down my body. Hands touched me from all sides. My body was moving independently of my will. I began to enunciate some wild and strange sounds that turned into hysterical screaming, then I fell to the ground, unconscious.

I woke up in my own bed around midnight, but I didn't remember how I got there; I was fully dressed except for my socks and shoes. I stumbled into the bathroom, sat in the bathtub and stayed there motionless, with the soft spray of warm water bringing me back to the world of tangible things. I took off my clothes, dried myself up and walked into the bedroom; I picked up the phone and dialed a telephone number that was written on a scrap of crumbled paper. "Marcos?" I said, "This is Miguel Saavedra. When is that trip you talked to me about?" The old man, in total disbelief, gave me all the information on how to get to Cuba; all the arrangements would be made by the Cuban Mission to the United Nations. I didn't have to do anything; they would contact me.

Antonio's funeral was an event of unparalleled importance in the exile community. Over ten thousand people attended the services: from women who knew him intimately, to political comrades, to the many people in the streets who knew him and loved him. Antonio proved to be as popular in death as he was in life. However, his death—sudden as it came—left an opaque veil of doubt and uncertainty. Some claimed he was killed by a jealous husband—others said that his death was the result of drug dealings. Others that he was killed by the Cuban government. There were even those who went as far as to say that Antonio's death was caused by members of an exile group. Thirty-one years of good living, but also thirty-one years of concern and dedication to the freedom of his country had come to nothing. Only his close relatives would bear the grief. The women would remember the good times. His friends would remember him when necessity so required. He may have been the quintessential young Cuban exile. Coming to the United States at an early age, he adapted to the American way only as far as necessary to be able to survive. He made a living. But more important than that, he was completely responsive to the needs, both spiritual and political, of his compatriots. He was alienated even from a great majority of his own people by his own people. Rejected by the present Cuba, but at the same time looked upon as an outsider by the old guard, the defeated members of the past generation, and considered by members of his own generation—those that had made it good, those that had reached the American dream, the affluent professionals who spoke a Cuban version of Spanish—that the newly arrived Cubans in the early sixties criticized so bitterly in the Puerto Ricans—as a prehistoric monster, a defeatist without a future. Antonio Perez Perez was a dichotomy within himself, a negation of himself. A lover and a revolutionary. A bon vivant and a patriot. A grass smoking moralist. His generation was indeed a lost generation. Many were killed. Many were jailed. Many had been won-over to the cause of inconsequence. The few who were left, scattered around the world—The United States, Europe and Latin America—were, ironically enough, the only ones who could possibly change conditions on the island. They understood and accepted the mistakes, and were willing to change. A strange group, indeed.

I had taken Antonio's death to heart. It was six months since we had met, and we had come to love each other as true friends; but more important, we had come to respect each other, to understand each other and accept each other's weaknesses. It's not an easy feat for some men to lower their defenses, to become vulnerable. Perhaps there weren't many who could have done that, most of our friends couldn't do it—Rodolfo, for one. I felt the weight of Antonio's convictions on my own shoulders.

I remembered one day when Antonio had paid me a visit. "Brother," he said, "there's something important I have to tell you. I've just come from a meeting. I've been talking for over ten hours. I've been fighting like a cornered cat. Goddamit. Listen, you're not going to believe this. We have formed a provisional government. I know it sounds premature. Well, I got the Department of Interior. It was not easy convincing them, but in the end they gave it to me."

I remember laughing at Antonio, whose face lit up as a young boy's on Christmas Day. That laughter hurts me now. It hurts me to have always been so supercilious, so pedant at times. All my philosophy, all my poetry, all my knowledge hurts me now as it did the day Antonio died. Antonio's death had occured only four days after the assassination of Jose Elias de la Torriente, a Cuban born CIA agent who had reportedly stolen some two million dollars that he had collected from the exile community for the liberation of Cuba, under the egocentric name of "The Torriente Plan." He was a certified public accountant who developed a great scheme to get rich in less than three years. Omega 7, a Cuban commando group, became the executioner that brought justice—in a Cuban exile manner—to those who favored the Castro government. In November 1979, Eulalio Jose Negrin, a member of the Committee of 75—who traveled to Cuba from the United States to dialogue with Fidel Castro—was also gunned down in Union City, New Jersey. I had decided to fly to Miami and find out for myself what had happened to Aldo. His wife confessed to me he had landed in Cuba with a shipment of arms that were secretly stashed on an island in the Bahamas. Aldo and nine of his revolutionary partners were to have landed in Las Villas province; from there they were to head for the Escambray Mountains, to attempt to overthrow the government. No one had heard from them since.

Someone from the Cuban Mission to the United Nations finally got in touch with me, giving me the details of my trip to Havana. I was to leave New Year's Eve for Canada where I would make the connecting flight to Cuba via the Cuban National Airlines. The celebration of the twentieth anniversary of the Cuban Revolution was no small matter. They were planning to make a big show of it; it was imperative to impress the non-aligned countries whose convention was going to be held in Havana later the same year. Before my departure for Cuba, I decided to go to Union City, New Jersey, the Cuban north east ghetto, untouched by the mechanism of time. The Orange and Black bus took me to Bergenline Avenue, with its furniture stores, butcher shops and vegetable stands; getting off the bus I saw, about half a block away,a man dressed in black—leather boots and leather jacket included— hitting and kicking an old man lying on the sidewalk. It was nearly three o'clock in the afternoon. I called out to the man—who looked like a German paratrooper out of a World War II documentary—to stop beating the old fellow. When the pseudo-nazi saw me running towards him, he gave the old man a last kick in the groin. I continued screaming, the assailant took off and I gave chase; a block away we were both running at full speed. I hadn't run in quite some time, but I didn't feel tired; as a matter of fact, I was enjoying it. For a moment I saw myself as a marathon runner; Bergenline Avenue became the Cuban countryside, the fields of Oriente where I grew up, running as a young, wild, tropical beast. I remembered—while losing ground to the Cuban nazi—when I was in boarding school, in Holguin; it was a clear afternoon like the one in Union City, when with three other friends I went off after Albertico Cardenas: he was a homosexual. About once a week we went after him with all the malice that twelve-year-old boys could muster; when we finally caught up with him, we wrestled him to the ground. With the high, wet grass as the only witness, we opened our flies, tempting Albertico with our little, wrinkled, pink penises. Albertico, who was a man of the world for a thirteen-year-old in the Cuba of the time, used to tickle each of us until we all ran back to the dormitory laughing and singing. One day, Albertico didn't get up for the morning bell; I went over to his bedside and asked him what was the matter.

"I am pregnant," he said, holding his belly with both hands.

"You can't be pregnant, don't be silly."

"But it hurts."

"I'll call the director."

"Yes, please. Tell him I can't get up, tell him I'm pregnant."

"I can't tell him that," I said rushing out.

"Tell him I'm pregnant," I heard him cry out in pain as I ran down the stairs.

The school director came to see Albertico, who proceeded to tell him the same story. The director took off his belt and gave the boy a horrible going over, hitting him right and left with his belt. "There will be no fags in my school," he cried at the boy with each swing of the belt. That afternoon, Albertico hung himself.

Almost totally out of breath, I came to a dead stop. If Bergenline Avenue seemed foreign to me a few minutes before, after reliving the impressionable experience of Albertico's death, I felt like Dante walking through the Inferno with an invisible Virgil. I felt totally locked within myself, attached to nothing, like the skin of an orange that simply gets thrown away. I began walking back; the old man was being helped up by some people who came out of a grocery store. My soul-searching trip had been a fiasco; I could do nothing but return to New York.

Since December 12th, freed Cuban political prisoners began arriving in Miami. They were, as the press called them, "The latest beneficiaries of the Cuban-American dialogue that had caused a bitter split in (Miami's) Cuban exile community." Castro's latest move had caught the exiles off-guard. They were utterly confused, frustrated, scared.

That evening, Ariadne called. It was the 22nd of December. She asked me to her house for dinner. Her parents had been invited out, and she wanted to cook for me; I accepted the invitation. Since the day of my poetry reading, when we met, I had wanted to be alone with her. She came from a lower middle class family; ironically enough, we both came from the same town in Oriente, although we had never met in Cuba. She had come to the United States at the age of seven. She was a graduate of New York University's philosophy department. At twenty-seven she was an assistant professor of philosophy. During her university studies, she kept active in an anti-Castro group. She was always—regardless of danger—in the frontlines. A few years before her skull had been fractured during a fight that broke out at Queens College after an speaking engagement by the senior delegate from the Cuban government to the United Nations. Ariadne had never been back to the island since she left with her parents. Like many other young men and women of her age, she was emotionally and intellectually obsessed with the cause of freedom for her country. Yes, they agreed the Revolution was necessary, but not to the point of becoming communist. They felt Castro had betrayed the Revolution.

Ariadne's house was full of Christmas decorations. There was a six-foot tree in a corner of the living room beautifully trimmed with large, red satin balls and very tiny white lights. At the foot of the tree, an incredible array of Christmas packages were wrapped in a bright red, glossy paper, with green bow and ribbon. Ariadne was cooking when I arrived. A record of Christmas carols in Spanish was playing on the phonograph. It was Fernando Albuerne, a well-known pre-Castro Cuban singer. I joined her in the kitchen, volunteering to make the salad. She opened a bottle of *Cidra El Gaitero*, a champagne like hard cider and typical Cuban drink for festive occasions. There was a roast in the oven. As she turned to go to the living room to turn the record over, she placed her glass on the dining table, and softly caressed my face. I took her hand and followed her to the living room. I was standing behind her as she changed the record. I unbuttoned her blouse; we undressed and lay down beside the Christmas tree. The red glow from the tree bathed her firm body. About twenty minutes after making love, we were still lying on the carpet beside the Christmas tree; she was leaning against the couch, her long legs rested on by back; I was lying face down, the right side of my face on top of my arm. I was staring at the tree, at the lights, at the satin balls; she was caressing my left arm.

"You know," she said, "I was brought up to make a man happy, to be a perfect woman. And look at me now, all I do is give a few hours of pleasure." I didn't answer, but acknowledge her remark by slightly turning my face towards her. "I was always like a little doll," she continued. "Imagine, I grew up in a house full of women, and I was the youngest; there was my mother, my sister, three of my aunts, and my grandmother." She bent her knees, and placed her feet against my torso. "I'm going to tell you something," she said, "that I've never told anyone." She remained silent for a few moments, pensive, bathed in melancholy. "When I was seven, someone took advantage of me." I tried not to appear shocked, calmly I just looked at her. "It was an uncle of mine—my mother's brother."

She was speaking softly, delicately, like a little girl; she didn't say anything else, so I asked her, "What happened?" I don't know if I really wanted to know, or if I simply wanted her to get it off her chest.

"There was a party in my house one night," she continued, "they were celebrating the triumph of the Revolution; everyone was in the backyard. It was very late at night, and I was very sleepy so I went upstairs. A few minutes later—I was already in bed— my bedroom door opened. It was my uncle; he was always playing with me, and bringing me presents. I used to love him very much." She paused, and with a faint smile she said, "I still love him. He sat on my bed, and began to touch me all over, and then he began kissing me; I was afraid, but I didn't know what to do. He was my uncle, and, I don't know, but I think I liked it. I couldn't shout or anything like that; I just let him touch me and kiss me. Little by little, he lay next to me, and then, he embraced me." She paused and stared at the Christmas tree, then she said, as if thinking out loud, "I still love him." Then, abruptly she changed the tone of her voice, "Did you know I had a sister?"

"No," I said.

"She was two years older than me, but we were born on the same day; we were very close, we had a very special relationship; we were always together. I don't remember for what reason, but one day we were separated, and we both got sick: I got a terrible fever, and my sister had some stomach disorder. We were always embracing each other. One day she became ill, and was taken to a hospital. A few months later, she died of cancer. I thought I was going to go mad." She lay next to me, on the carpet, resting her head on her left hand. "When we applied for a visa to leave the country, we were sent to a farm in Pinar del Rio, but they didn't tell our family where they had sent us. My sister and I arrived at the farm, and since they didn't expect us there, they didn't have a place for us to sleep, nor anything to eat. We were taken to a wooden building where they kept the tobacco for us. For the first few days they didn't give us anything to eat; in the afternoon we went to a camp nearby and ate the leftovers. We worked from six in the morning to six in the evening. There were a lot of lesbians in the farm, so my sister, another girl and I used to watch out for each other; when two of us slept, the third was on guard. We had to work even if we were ill. Even after I became ill, I had to continue working until day, while carrying a sack of tobacco, I collapsed; it was then I lost a kidney. I remember that sometimes when our family came to visit, if we were working we were forbidden to speak to them, or even to acknowledge them; if we did, they would deny us our visa. They used to insult us with the filthiest obscenities, we couldn't do anything or say anything; if we did, they would deny us our visa. I was sixteen then. To be able to visit our parents we had to fulfill a work quota that was so high that I was never able to visit my mother during all the time I was working at that farm. I spent my teenage years waiting, always waiting for a letter, a telegram, a telephone call, anything. During the night, some girls used to have attacks of hysteria, and the screaming was unbearable. The day that Fidel announced—I think it was in '65— that Cuba was a free country, there was a national feast; everyone took to the streets. People were singing, shouting, 'Hey, did you get your permit yet?' It was like a huge party. The next day, however, he announced the draft for people from fifteen to forty-five; the feast end. There was a little cow on television, her name was Matilda. Whenever she appeared you would hear a little song:

> Matilda comes and goes,
> she sees, she hears, she knows.

She was a little cow from the Committee for the Defense of the Revolution. She was everywhere. There was also Prudencio, a bear, that was in charge of the traffic; he also had a little song:

> Prudencio the bear
> Says drive and beware;
> Watch out for pedestrians.

When food got scarce, the black market began; a man used to come to our neighborhood on a bicycle with two large tin cans tied to the back, full of meat. At one time there was no milk and all one could get for breakfast was a steak, nothing else. Everybody got sick after a while. At the beginning of the Revolution, the children who had been going to catholic school stayed home. Their parents thought that the new system wouldn't last, and they didn't want their children to go to a state run school. We were out of school for about two years; until one day Fidel announced that education was obligatory, so we had to attend a public school. There was no place to go to have fun, so we began to have parties; the communist youth began to come to our parties and smashed our records. Later they broke the record players, so that was the end of our get-togethers. Do you know that after the triumph of the Revolution my grandfather never spoke again? He used to sit and read the newspaper or listen to the radio, but he wouldn't say a word. He was like Rafael del Junco, the character in that soap opera, *El Derecho de Nacer*, who was the catalyst, on whom the outcome of the story depended; and who, although episodes came and went would not say a word. My grandfather did just like Rafael del Junco; he died without ever speaking another word. One day we got our visa, and I felt so happy, but I couldn't help being sad thinking of the friends we had made during the two years we worked at the farm who would have to stay behind." She turned her face away, then she cried, "Oh, my God! The meat must have burnt!" She got up, wiping tears from her eyes, and ran to the kitchen. I remained lying on the carpet, looking at the blinking white lights on the Christmas tree. "It's all right," she cried from the kitchen, "I got it just in time!"

A DANCER'S UTOPIA

During the Ten Year's War—1868 to 1878—there was an ex-slave revolutionary leader, his name was Guillermon. He was quite successful in his campaigns against the better trained and equipped Spanish army. He had actually become a legendary figure. After each battle, when they camped out for the night, Guillermon would organize a dance to relieve the fatigue and suffering of his men.

Throughout Cuban history, dancing has been one of the great passions of the people of the island. Cubans would give up anything for a dance; they would forget everything while dancing; they would do anything to dance.

In his inaugural speech on May 20th, 1902, the first President of the Republic of Cuba, Estrada Palma, addressed his compatriots:

> "The Americans weren't sure whether to put us Cubans in charge of the government, thinking that we couldn't get serious about anything. According to them, everything for us is a party. We solve everything by making fun, by dancing. But we Cubans are a serious people. Don't you agree?"
>
> The audience shouted in unison, "*¡Sí, señor!*"
>
> Estrada Palma continued, "We Cubans have the right to guide our own lives because our spirit is that of liberty. Do you agree?"
>
> "*¡Sí, señor!*"
>
> "Because we have been oppressed for too long. Do you agree?"
>
> "*¡Sí, señor!*"
>
> "Do you agree?"
>
> "*¡Sí, señor!*"
>
> "Do you agree?"

"*¡Sí, señor!*"

Everyone began clapping their hands, moving in their seats to the rhythm of the continuing exchange.

"Do you agree?"

"*¡Sí, señor!*"

They all got up and began to dance their way to independence.

Well, the dance continues here and now; the beat is the same, but not the feeling. No, too much has happened in seventy-seven years. Too many dead men and women, and illusions and hopes.

A strange music is playing now. I thought it may be time for me to get on the dance floor and show what I could do. On the day of my departure, I received a letter from a friend to whom Alicia had confided my plans.

Alicia and I were both the same age. She had left Cuba after spending a year at a school work camp in the countryside, on her fifteenth birthday. The twelve months of physical and moral abuse had left deep scars on the camp's two hundred or so teenaged girls, of whom Alicia was one. One day she was told that she was being deported; because her parents had had close ties to the Batista government, they would have to stay behind. On her arrival in Florida she was sent to a temporary camp for the exiled girls set up in Opa Locka. This second detention, even if not as degrading as the first, was nothing short of heartbreaking. Now, at thirty-three, she was still attempting to make sense of her life. Her smile, always sad, never really managed a full expression, even on the happiest of moments. In the taxi, on my way to the airport, I read her letter:

"The first thing I must tell you is that I love you for what you are, my dear brother of so many years, so many distances, so many trips and so many silent moments. I love you very much. I love you with a pain which I cannot explain. Perhaps soon you will be breathing my air, your air; standing on my land, your land; feeling on your face the warmth of my sun; walking along my streets."

I had to stop reading. Out the car window I could see the indifferent gray of the factories and of the sadness of the two-story family houses. My eyes traveled along the perfect curves of the vowels, the fluid n's and l's. I could hear her honey-like voice: "You are the Cuban exile; you're all of us, you with your longing and your endless nostalgia. You're always in my mind like a shield, like a wall I use to protect myself. Love, Alicia."

The Eastern Airlines terminal was very crowded; there's nothing worse than a holiday at an airport. An hour later I was in

Montreal, Canada. I was driven by car to Minabel Airport, where I would board Cubana de Aviacion flight #481, destination Havana.

Setting foot on the Cuban plane itself was a strange feeling. It took me back twenty years when together with my family I became an exile on a plane just like this one. I was thirteen then. The rest of the passengers on our Havana-bound flight were, for the most part, Canadian tourists, and a few old Cuban couples who had to stay in Canada overnight as a security measure. The stewardesses were quite pleasant; they served us Cuban rum, Cuban cigars, Cuban souvenirs and Cuban smiles. The flight was a return trip for me, a necessary return. I was returning home. Ideology aside, it was still home. Was I closer to Havana than to Miami? I couldn't tell. In the mail, together with Alicia's letter, I had received another letter. It was from Sonia, a friend who was studying in Spain. For some reason which I didn't understand, she was a member of the "Group of 75" who had had a dialogue with Castro. She had befriended members of the Cuban delegation in Madrid; she had traveled to Cuba by invitation of the government and had even met with Castro at private parties. On one of the trips from Spain to Havana, she had stopped in New York to see her family; she took that opportunity to pick up some of my poetry books to take with her to Cuba.

In her small and scientific handwriting, she had decided to confess something she had known for a long time: Luis Vega, my friend from Miami was working for the Cuban government. It was he who had recommended me for the supposed cultural exchange; it was he who had Marcos, the old man, follow me through some of his contacts that had infiltrated the Cuban exile groups. Luis Vega was able to get me invited to their meetings. I had been planted in the exile community by a Cuban agent. During a party at the Cuban Embassy in Madrid, Sonia had overheard someone joking about how they had been able to get an exiled writer to work for them without his being aware that he was being used. They had created an image for me, one they would later destroy it: a tropical version of the cold war.

After reading the letter, I couldn't eat or drink anything. What would be my next step? I had no idea. One thing was certain, it was not a round-trip. From then on the flight seemed to last an eternity. For a moment I forgot where it was I was going. It was the stewardess' voice that awoke me: "Ladies and gentlemen, welcome to José Martí Airport, in Havana, Cuba." A mixture of anguish and happiness came over me. We had landed quite far from the main terminal, which seemed to be overflowing with Cuban exiles returning home to see their families; it was a pathetic scene, everyone was crying.

One of the benefits of being a guest of the government is the forgoing of all custom's formalities. A man in his fifties and a woman in her twenties were waiting for me. They picked up my luggage and we drove off in a white Alfa Romeo.

My hosts were making every effort to make me feel at home; they would point out places of interest, tell me anecdotes and ask me about my feelings upon returning home. Before driving to the hotel, they gave me a small and private tour of Havana, a city that I vaguely remembered from childhood; a city through which I had walked, countless times through photographs; a city I knew from other peoples recollections; from invented images and lost illusions of so many people I knew who were exiled in the United States, yet continued to live in Havana. All I could do was to take deep breaths of fresh air, "My air," as Alicia had said in her letter; I felt the warmth of "my sun" and heard the voice of the city, "my voice." That evening, there was a reception for me, so I was finally driven to the hotel so that I could rest. How could I? It was January 1st, 1979. I had twenty-four hours in which to get ready; twenty-four hours to find myself. My search would end one way or another; my life would finally be defined. The lobby of the Havana Libre Hotel sounded like the dining room at the United Nations. American tourists, Eastern European dignitaries, African students, Latin American writers mingled in a euphoric maze which resembled more a Brazilian Carnival than a political celebration. Cuba was in fashion. Madison Avenue was going at full force in Havana. The Cuban exiles were the only ones not directly participating, but the government was taking care of that. The release of political prisoners, the reunification of families, and finally the integration of intellectuals, still hostile or apprehensive, with the New Cuba. I was the first link of that final stage.

My room was on the sixth floor, #606. There were fresh flowers, a bottle of Cuban rum, a box of Romeo and Julieta cigars, current Cuban literary magazines. Someone knocked at the door. It was a man carrying a tray with an ice bucket, a bottle of water, and a package wrapped in brown paper under his arm. He entered, closed the door behind him and placed the tray on the dresser. He offered to make me a drink. "This is room six zero six," he said. I looked at him puzzled. "Six," he said, emphasizing the number. "I don't have much time," he continued, "this room is the only one that is not bugged. We made sure of that. I am Pedro. I'm your contact."

"You're what?" I asked.

"Luis Vega is on our side," he explained, "we've been waiting for you for a long time. Here, we're all being watched. It's impossible for us to do anything; we needed someone from outside, someone who could get close to Fidel."

I had to interrupt, "Wait, listen."

"I have to go, or they'll get suspicious. Here is the book. Ariadne spoke to you about it. It's the collected poems of José Martí." He handed me the book and started for the door. I made a vain attempt to call his attention. The door closed after him. I placed the book back on top of the dresser, without taking off the brown paper wrapper.

Around five, Felicia Estrada, my female escort, arrived. We rode, in the same Alfa Romeo that had driven us from the airport, to a beautiful ranch on the outskirts of Havana. We were the last to arrive. It seemed as if everyone that was important in Cuba was present, except Fidel. He was busy preparing his speech for the celebration. A few years back he could improvise a speech and speak for hours. Now he had to write them. A couple of hours later, I had met almost all of the two hundred people gathered there, including José Luis Larriaga, the famed Colombian novelist and Leo Riccardi, the Argentine writer, plus several other poets, novelists and playwrights from Cuba and Latin America. Most of the afternoon was spent talking about literature. It seemed as if I was doing most of the talking. They all were very curious about me. An exiled Cuban writer in Havana? What was I doing there? What was I writing about at the time? Was there a Cuban literature outside of Cuba? Our dear friends from South America had no idea we existed. It's as if we were some sort of strange, prehistoric animal. I assured them that Cuban literature was alive and well in the United States and Europe, that they should make an effort to catch up with us. Anyhow, the next day at the celebration of the twentieth anniversary of the Revolution, they could get a preview since I was to read a poem I had written for the occasion.

Around nine in the evening we left. Felicia wanted to show me Havana by night.

We had dinner at La Bodeguita del Medio, and then went on to see the show at Tropicana. I had been with Felicia for over eight hours during which we didn't speak a word of politics. She spoke to me about the people in Cuba. I spoke to her about the people outside of Cuba. Neither of us wanted to prove anything. We simply wanted to give each other information. We wanted to know each other.

I liked her very much. She was intelligent, concerned, tender and beautiful. She reminded me of Cyndie, the Puerto Rican girl of my New York dreams. She had long hair and very dark skin. She had graduated from the University of Havana, and was working for *Casa de las Americas* magazine, besides teaching literature at a high school. She also went to the countryside on weekends to work as stage manager of a theater group.

Around three in the morning, we were walking along the Malecon. In spite of everything, Havana is a magical city. The view of the bay from the Malecon into the bay is breathtaking. The streets were almost deserted except for a few tourists walking back to their hotel. Felicia and I stood, facing each other. A cool breeze caressed her hair which glistened in the moonlight. Gracefully she turned and began walking. She smiled at me and said, "Let's walk." Then she lowered her voice and continued, "Act naturally. We are being watched." She smiled. I didn't know what to do; I simply followed her, smiling back at her and then she stunned me. "Aldo is dead. He and the other men were caught on the beach when they landed in Las Villas. They were all shot right there. There are many acts of sabotage taking place all through the island. There are many dissatisfied veterans of the African wars. There are many enlisted men going AWOL. Young soldiers steal small weapons from the military and trade them to dissidents on the black market for food, tape recorders and radios. However, it has been impossible to get near Fidel. No one ever sees him."

"How do you know about Aldo? That I know him, I mean?" I asked her as we kept on walking.

"My brother was one of his contacts."

I stopped walking, she pulled me by the hand and continued. "Don't worry, I won't turn you in."

Our car approached, and she let go of my hand. I was taken back to the hotel as Felicia, very formally, talked to me about the next day's festivities.

I waited for sunrise on the balcony of my room not being able to sleep. A Cuban sunrise is nothing short of breathtaking, it's like a painting by Turner, a Mozart sonata, the laughter of a child.

Since early in the morning, the city was bursting with movement. People walking to and from, cars, army trucks, soldiers. Around eight o'clock, I went inside to shave and take a shower. The sleepless night was beginning to get to me, and I wanted to be in good form for the occasion. The phone rang while I was still in the shower. Dripping water, I went over to answer it. It was room

service; they were bringing me breakfast in five minutes. I hung
up and went into the bathroom to dry myself.

I combed my hair back, as I used to do in my Don Juan days. I
put on a white suit and a collarless, light blue shirt. I had breakfast,
took some papers from my suitcase and my notebook. I gave a last
glance to the mirror and noticed the book on the dresser. I picked
it up, removed the wrapper and placed it under my arm together
with my notebook. In the lobby, the man who had met me at
the airport was waiting for me. Felicia wasn't there. He greeted
me and directed me to the car. The sky was starting to get dark.
On our way to the Plaza de la Revolucion, where the celebration
was to take place, a tropical storm broke out. The thousands of
people who had been gathering there for hours, ran to take cover
from the rain. We remained in the car. Not long after, the rain
subsided. The crowd began filing back. Atop a large, high platform
members of the government hierarchy began taking their places.
I was among the guests who were also on the platform. Music
was playing. Small paper flags were waved by the crowd. Planes
were flying overhead. Someone started testing the microphones.
Suddenly, I heard a commotion. People began cheering. Fidel had
just arrived. He was coming from behind the platform. When
he became visible to the crowd, shouts of, "Fidel! Fidel!" were
heard. He waved to them smiling. I was introduced to him, and
to the other people that I had not yet met. A few minutes later the
celebration began. Raul Castro opened the meeting. There were
several speeches after that. About two hours later, the Minister of
Culture introduced me. The crowd applauded, waving the little
paper flags.

I greeted the mass audience, and proceeded to read:

> This shall be a historic silence,
> A rhapsody of distant cries:
> Multiple songs that never found a voice.
> Verses between cities,
> Between repeated stories,
> Repeated deaths,
> Repeated fantasies
> That come and go like windy dreams.
> We are the children of lament
> With an infinite guilt
> That some still consider necessary.

Without finishing the poem, I put down the paper from which I
was reading, knowing that the adventure always has a bad ending.

It was neither an appropriate role, nor the appropriate place for a poet.

With the same movement by which I put down the piece of paper, I picked up the dummy book of verses, opened it and took out the .45 caliber automatic it concealed. I turned around to where Castro had been sitting, only to realize that the supreme leader of the Cuban Revolution wasn't there any longer.

I felt so utterly ridiculous standing there, with a gun in my hand and no one to shoot at.

As the bullets began showering up on me from all over the platform, as my body jumped back from the impact, as I felt a cold in the center of my head, as my senses slowly left my body, as the crowd ran and cried in terror, as my head finally hit the wooden platform, as life ebbed from me, a smile came over what was left of my face. At that instant, I knew I was home.

ROUND TRIP

At that moment, he woke up. He always woke up precisely at that moment, when Miguel fell to the ground with his head blown off. He glanced across the hall at the typewriter on top of the desk. In it was the last page of the novel, where he narrated the death of the young poet.

He got up, went to the next room, and read the last paragraph he had written; then he returned to the bedroom. Deliberately he picked up the phone, and dialed the number that was written on a piece of paper, on top of the dresser.

"Marcos? This is Miguel. When is that flight?"

They wanted Miguel to be in Havana on December 31st. Marcos would call him back with the details.

The circle was closed. Virgo had been faithful to its moons.

EPILOGUE

Her grandmother had died in New York on Mother's Day, while receiving the "The Cuban Mother of the Year" tribute. Her body, however, had been taken to Miami for burial. "I don't want to die here," she is supposed to have said. Preferably, she would have wanted for her bones put to rest in Cuban soil. That was impossible, so Miami was the next best thing. She, the granddaughter, was a college student; modern in her ways, astute, creative, with a jungle of hair on her head and a six-part color harmony on her dress.

The day I went to see her, a week after the funeral, she received me in a two-piece black suit and a blouse with a red flower print. Her hair was pulled back and she was wearing no make-up. I pictured her in a small town near Havana, around 1940, as the girl-next-door; perhaps just as her grandmother had looked when she was young.

When I was nine, I went to visit my mother's brother at his house in the country. Near my uncle's house, I saw a man standing underneath a tree, staring at the birds flying from one branch to another. When he noticed me standing behind him, he turned around, smiled and said, "Cuban birds never really leave their nest, they just fly around a little." I guess peasants have their wisdom.